THE DARKNESS WE CRAVE

TOGETHER WE FALL BOOK 1

KATIE MAY

Edited by Meg West

Cover Design by Melody Simmons

❀ Created with Vellum

To my sister. Sorry I always have to kill you off. Love you.

CONTENTS

PROLOGUE

*T*he only friend I ever had was killed.

You would think that I would remember his death in vivid detail, but I don't. At least, not consciously. My therapist said that it was my way of coping with the loss.

I do, however, remember the day I met him. Like a distorted tattoo, the details of that day have permanently imprinted themselves into my brain. One could best compare our meeting to a fairytale. There was a girl and a boy, a knight and a fearful child. You see, this is where our story varies from most others: he was weak, and I was strong. I had never been the damsel-in-distress type of girl, and he had never been the knight-in-shining-armor type of guy. Our pasts were too atypical to create such stereotypes.

The day I met him, the weather had been uncharacteristically cold, and the trees seemed to be cooperating, their branches leafless. If anything, it was beginning to look more like fall than the previous months had displayed. I was terrified my butt was going to freeze off, and I would be forced to poop out of my mouth (Nanny #1 had a huge imagination).

Daddy and Mommy had been fighting again. I remember

that detail, but I can't recall what the fight was about. I remember, he called her a lot of nasty names, and she retorted with another guy's name, declaring that he was "better" than my father. Of course, my innocent brain thought she was talking about cooking or some shit like that. Well, in my defense, it turns out the other guy *did* know how to take care of a muffin, if you know what I mean.

My eyes flickered nervously between Mommy and Daddy; my small hands held my favorite doll in a death-grip. I wore a new outfit my nanny (yes, the one who told me I'd shit from my mouth) bought me - a white, billowing number with a contrasting red bow. She had plaited my hair into two braids, too, and I felt beautiful for the first time in my life. All I had ever wanted to be was the little girl my mommy and daddy loved and wanted.

"Mommy! Daddy!" I pleaded, my little voice trembling. "Please stop fighting."

Daddy looked at me as if he had just realized I was in the room with them. Instead of apologizing like I expected at getting caught in an argument, he appeared almost enraged. Even back then, he didn't like me interrupting him. He didn't like me doing anything, really, besides smiling like the pretty puppet he wanted when he birthed me.

Before I could even think to scream, he had grabbed one of my braids and dragged me outside.

My knees had hit the grass, small rocks and other unsavory substances digging into my skin as my dress rode up. The poor dress itself was stained a deep brown and an almost garnet red.

Blood, I realized numbly. My blood.

And Dolly, well, Daddy hadn't been gentle with her. Stuffing covered the grass, mixing with the stream of blood from my legs. The sight would cause any psychopathic pedophile to orgasm.

I stared at my doll for a long moment, barely hearing my dad's cuss words and threats aimed towards his six-year-old daughter. I didn't even process it when he slapped me across the face.

No, my eyes remained fixed on Dolly. She couldn't be gone, not Dolly. Who would have tea parties with me or cuddle with me when I became scared at night?

I didn't cry as I stared at her maimed body. I was too numb for that, and still, somehow innately I knew that she wasn't real. You couldn't mourn an inanimate object.

No, it would take a few more years, not until I was thirteen, to understand what mourning meant. But I wasn't the savior during that point of my life. I was the murderer.

Looking back at my interaction with Dolly, I found it ironic that I lost something important to me the same day I gained the best friend I ever had.

Sniffling, I watched my dad's back retreat into the house until the door slammed shut, leaving me alone and outside as if I was nothing more than discarded trash. Maybe that was all I had ever been to him.

It took me a few tries to scrambled to my feet. My body shook from my dad's unexpected aggression. Looking back, I suppose you could say that my dad's anger was the only constant in my life.

Piles of leaves littered across the grass and sidewalk, crunching underneath my sock-clad feet. I wrapped my arms around myself, attempting to ease the sting in my arms. The chill from the howling wind caused goosebumps to erupt on my flesh.

With no purpose or destination in mind, I walked. All I knew was that I wanted to get as far away as possible from the two people who were supposed to provide me with unconditional love. Of course, these thoughts only came to me later when I was older. All I remember at the time was wondering why Daddy didn't love me. Why had he hit me? Did I do something wrong? Why was I a failure as a daughter, even wearing my beautiful new dress?

I wasn't aware how far I had walked until I stumbled upon a gated playground.

A school, I realized almost dumbly. Like where the kids on TV go.

I had never been to school before. For as long as I could remember, Daddy kept me in purposeful isolation and therefore, homeschooled. He didn't want me to have friends.

Kids climbed the jungle gym, played tag in a field, and swung on the swings. The sight seemed almost ethereal, and my little brain attempted to process everything at once.

For a brief moment, jealousy speared my chest. I was the girl who had everything, yet ironically, my isolation grew more pronounced in the presence of people – at least the people my parents *allowed* me to associate with, namely stuffy children of business executives.

I simply stared at the kids in awe. I didn't want to join them; I wanted to *be* them.

My searching eyes landed on a figure surrounded in a sandbox. She was bent over a toy truck, her dark hair cascading down to her knees. She appeared dainty compared to the boys surrounding her, and I couldn't see her face.

Moving along the fence line, I planted myself in front of the sandbox, metal separating me from the elfin figure. I caught the end of the taller boy's speech.

"…freak. Why don't you choke on sand?"

"Hey!" I yelled before I could rethink my decision (because, really, when did I ever think things through?). I balled my hands into fists and banged them against the fence. The rattling sound, more than my voice, startled the bullies. The one I initially heard speak narrowed his eyes at me.

"What are you doing here? You don't even go to school here!"

I tried to keep my voice strident, like my father always did. "Stop picking on her, and I'll leave!"

For some reason, my words sent the boys into another fit of laughter.

"See, freak? Even a stranger thinks you're a girl!" A new voice retorted, poking the long-haired figure in the back. In my mind, I referred to this boy as Short Stack. No reason, really, except for the fact that his face looked like someone had smeared syrup on it, stuck cement to said syrup, and then came and ripped the cement off his face. Yup, he was *that* ugly, and my nanny's vivid imagination had rubbed off on me.

It was when the sandbox-child turned around to hit away Short Stack's finger did I realize that he wasn't a girl, but a guy. He had decidedly masculine, if not slightly cherubic, features. His haunted eyes stared at me with such sadness and betrayal that my heart began to pound an erratic rhythm in my chest.

"Leave him alone," I said, proud I kept my voice steady. My eyes never left the long-haired boy's face.

"What are you going to do about it, girl?" One of the bullies, I didn't see which, taunted.

There was no way I would beat these boys in a physical fight, but I had one thing they didn't. An abundant knowledge of useless facts that no six-year-old should know.

"Do you know who I am?" I asked, straightening my spine. It did very little to add height to my short frame, but it made me feel somewhat imperious to these bullies.

"A girl?" Bully 1 - let's call him Turd Wiper – asked, oh so original with his gibe.

"I am the world's youngest doctor," I lied, crossing my

arms over my chest. Short Stack snorted, but Bully 3 - Not Relevant Enough to Name - looked slightly anxious.

"Bull crap," Turd Wiper said.

"It's true. And if you don't leave him alone, I will pull out your mitochondria, and you will die."

That big word threw them off guard. Three sets of eyes flitted to my face with varying degrees of horror.

"You can't – you can't do that!" one of them stuttered. I believe it was Not Relevant that spoke.

"The mitochondria are the powerhouse of the cell. If you don't have it, you'll die."

"But-"

"And I'll also give you hydrocephalus!" The boys shifted uneasily. "And your heads will explode."

Looking back, I don't know if it was my nonsense words or my slightly sardonic smile that did it. Maybe it was the sincerity in which I threatened to murder them. Either way, the boys ran away as if a hound from hell chased them, nipping at their heels.

"You run away!" I yelled after them. "And don't let the swing hit you on the way out!"

I waited until they were out of sight – no doubt tattling to a teacher – before turning towards the boy.

"Are you okay?" I asked somewhat tentatively. I was afraid that he'd run from me too.

While he didn't run, he didn't address me either. He continued to stare up at me as if I was an exotic specimen, a zebra in a flock of sheep.

"My name's Adelaide," I said after a moment of uncomfortable silence. "What's your name?"

At first, I thought that he wasn't going to answer, but he mumbled something inarticulate under his breath.

"Ducky?" I asked, afraid I had heard him wrong. When he didn't correct me, I smiled down at him. I'm sure I looked like a mess – what, with my disheveled hair and blood-stained dress, I was probably giving out The Ring vibes – but Ducky didn't seem to mind. He actually smiled back at me.

"Well, Ducky, I would stick around, but I have a feeling those jerks will be back and get me in trouble."

Ducky's face fell as if disappointed that I wasn't staying. It suddenly occurred to me that I didn't want to leave either. There was such wistfulness in his face that I knew mirrored my own. We were both broken souls in desperate need of a friend.

"How about I come back tomorrow?" I said. "I'll meet you here?"

The smile that lit up his face was glorious.

That same smile haunted me for years after his death.

CHAPTER 1

$\mathcal{M}$r. Fuckadoodledoo-picklesucker-buttlicker was leering at me. Again. I mentally tallied the number of times I caught his penetrating eyes turned in my direction over the last hour. Fifty-two. He had eye raped me *fifty-two* times in a span of sixty minutes.

Stiffening in my seat, I attempted to pay attention to my father across from me and ignore Mr. Buttlicker. D.O.D. – Dear Old Dad – had his peppered hair trimmed so it cascaded neatly to his shoulders. He wore a gray suit that seemed to accentuate the blue in his eyes. Some might've considered him a handsome man once, if they found ice-cold asshole statues handsome. Seriously, the man was a dick. He even put Buttlicker to shame in the whole creeper-asshole department.

We had arrived at the restaurant only a few minutes earlier, traveling immediately from the conference room to the elegant restaurant in the basement of the resort. The only word adequate to describe such a room was golden. I know, not the most eloquent description, but a golden sheen seemed to paint everything, from the intricately carved wood work to the golden flowers canvasing the wall. It was almost nauseating.

"I appreciate you taking the time to meet with us," D.O.D. said, for probably the billionth time that evening. I resisted the urge to roll my eyes. Buttlicker had as much choice in the matter as I did – needless to say, none at all.

"It's always a pleasure doing business with you," Buttlicker responded stiffly. His tone suggested, though, that he found it anything but pleasurable. Daddy tended to evoke fear in his clients.

"What looks good?" D.O.D. asked, scanning the menu.

And cue...

"I can think of one thing." Buttlicker's gaze flickered appreciatively over my body, and I resisted the urge to shiver. He made me feel naked, despite the fact I purposefully wore a modest black number with a pearl necklace strung tightly across my neck. The guy also seemed to be forgetting the fact that he was thirty-some years older than my own age of seventeen.

A reminder, my friends, pedophilia is a punishable offense.

My mother made a sound as if she heard Buttlicker's comment and found it as repulsive as I had...wait, no. She was just ogling our waiter's backside while simultaneously touching Mr. Dickhead's – aka our head of security's – knee underneath the table. Like seriously? Did the woman not realize I sat directly beside her, clearly able to see her hand trailing upwards towards no-no land. Dear Lord. The woman was going to be the death of me.

As I thought this, Buttlicker gave me a smile that he must've thought was seductive but came across as more of a constipated grimace.

Correction. *He* was going to be the death of me.

The waiter, that my mother so shamelessly gaped at,

stopped at our table, and my mouth nearly fell from its hinges.

The guy was gorgeous. Like ridiculously gorgeous. His ash blond hair was disheveled, as if he had run his hand through it one too many times. His eyes, a vibrant off-set blue that seemed to heighten an already arresting face, sparkled as if he was the only one privy to an inside joke. Even his cheekbones – oh sweet baby Jesus, those cheek bones – were chiseled and rose high on his face.

And. He. Had. Dimples.

My one weakness.

"Good afternoon. My name is Asher, and I'll be taking care of you this evening."

"Is that a promise?" My mother batted her eyelashes at him, and I felt my own eyes widen in horror.

"Dammit, mother," I hissed. If it was possible, and I didn't think it was, D.O.D.'s expression darkened further. If he hated one thing, it was the attention his wife gave other males. Of course, D.O.D. made an exception for Dickhead the guard, but that could've been because he was banging him too.

I touched my pearl necklace, a reminder of what I could gain with a little blackmail.

If only it could *rid* me of such nuisances, say the Buttlicker licking his buttlicking lips beside me.

I wanted to apologize to the waiter for my mother's crude, though unsurprising, behavior. However, I knew the gesture would be futile. D.O.D. was not only the owner of this ostentatious restaurant, but the entire resort. And a few other not-so-legal enterprises that I probably shouldn't mention.

Gorgeous kept his smile pleasant though his eyes dimmed marginally. He looked embarrassed by my mother's outburst, but how could he not? She basically implied that he was a prostitute to hire, despite the fact that he could only be a year or two older than myself.

"I'd like the chicken alfredo," I said quickly. A pathetic attempt, I'll admit, to ease the awkward tension, but it seemed to have the desired effect. D.O.D. let out a breath I hadn't realized he had been holding, and mother's face contorted into a scowl. She really didn't like it when I interrupted her flirt sessions, as she so liked to call them. Gorgeous's eyes flickered to me, his relief obvious.

And then they stayed there.

I knew he what held his gaze. It was the same thing that everybody else saw, the same thing I saw when I looked into the mirror. A girl that was almost ethereal in beauty with brown, curly hair and a porcelain-like face. Bright red lips and a cute, button nose. And my eyes – a color that seemed to be a mixture of violet and blue, like the light at the crack of dawn where the sun had yet to set and the moon had yet to disappear completely.

Did nobody see how haunted these eyes were? How my lips were constantly turned down into a frown? How the makeup was barely able to conceal the bruises marring the perfect skin?

Did anybody care?

Asher continued to stare at me, a blond brow lifting slightly. His mouth opened before snapping closed again. I couldn't understand the expression on his face.

Buttlicker also must've noticed the attention the waiter gave me, for he rested his hand possessively on my knee. I winced, shifting away from the man who made me squeamish. One reprimanding stare from my father had me cowering and leaning closer towards Buttlicker.

It was a choice between two evils. With Buttlicker, I knew that I would survive whatever he had in store for me. With my father, I could never be too sure.

Gorgeous' gaze hardened as he surveyed my father and then Buttlicker, but he didn't comment. Smart move.

"And what can I get you?" Asher asked sharply, turning towards the slimy man still gripping my knee as if his life depended on it. Yup. That was going to leave a nasty bruise there.

Great. Another one added to the inventory.

Mental me could barely contain her eye roll.

"Did you say something?" Buttlicker asked, turning his attention from Asher to me. This time I did roll my eyes, both physically and mentally (if there's such thing as rolling your eyes mentally. I'm not exactly sure, but I pictured myself rolling my eyes inside my mind. Does that count?)

"I didn't say anything," I huffed, glaring a hole at my menu. I had a tendency to speak my mind. Literally. Therapist 1 called it a defense mechanism for my traumatic childhood – whatever the hell that means. Therapist 2 said it was a way for me to express myself. Therapist 3 just chuckled and called me an idiot (I don't believe Therapist 3 was an *actual* therapist), but Therapist 4 admitted that it was not uncommon for trauma patients, when facing isolation, to find comfort in their own thoughts. Thus, my inner monologues and rumblings often turned into outer monologues and rumblings. You can imagine how embarrassing it can be at times, especially with my tendency to create nicknames.

Asher continued taking orders around the table, and I half expected my mother to make a smartass comment along the lines of "I'll have you for supper" or something dumb like that. I was pleasantly surprised when she only made a passing comment about having "the Asher special for dessert". That was real progress for my mother.

I wonder if his last name is Gorgeous? Then I wouldn't feel as creepy calling him Gorgeous. Asher Gorgeous. Hmmm. Fitting.

It took me a moment to realize that all eyes were on me,

including the stunning waiter who directed his blinding smile at me.

I tried to recall what I had just thought, and obviously said, and my cheeks flamed with the realization of what transpired.

"Shit."

Kill me now.

"Tempting," D.O.D. said, taking a sip of his water. His expression was as severe as his eyes. I had the distinct feeling that he wasn't joking. Great. Just what I wanted.

"So, about those Red Sox?" I interjected quickly. Though, in the middle of winter, I doubted that baseball had started up again. Sports. Sports were always a good topic of conversation with men. Asher, moving from our table to the next, smirked at me. He had no doubt heard my comment and found it amusing. What can I say? I have that effect on people.

Conversation, thankfully, steered away from the whole me-dying-of-mortification-thing and Red Sox to more work-related material. Taxes and employees and the whole stimulating shebang. They didn't talk about any of their, for back of better term, *illegal* enterprises, though not that I blamed them. I wondered how that conversation would go.

"I was wondering, how much you have been selling those illegal guns for?"

"The same amount as I have been selling my coke." Or pot. Or marijuana. Or whatever the hell they were up to these days.

D.O.D. had insisted that I take part in the business.

"You're no longer a little girl," he had told me sternly. "You have to start training to take over the family business."

I snorted. Family business made me think of a sweet, loving family that laughed as they fixed their shop and then came home to meals around the dinner table. I'm pretty sure that most *family businesses* didn't involve over a hundred shell companies, connections with the mafia, and a date with the drug lord of Mexico. Running the "family business" sounded about as appealing to me as stabbing my eye repeatedly with a rusted spoon would've been. Needless to say, it wasn't appealing.

Still, I behaved like the good girl, the good daughter, that my parents wanted me to be. It wasn't so much to please them as it was to protect myself. When I was good, when I listened and obeyed, they had no reason to punish me.

No reason to send people like Buttlicker to my room.

The mere thought made me tremble as if I had been electrocuted. My hand absently pulled at my sweater sleeves until they covered my hands.

It wasn't long before our meal came, though it was a different waiter from the one earlier that delivered it. Great. The *one* guy that I actually found attractive, my family had to go and scare him away.

I shouldn't have been surprised. The longest relationship I had...well, that lasted approximately two days. In kindergarten.

You see, I had a little problem (yes, even more of a problem than talking to myself). It involved people. And it involved my lack of talking to them. To some, I came across as a complete and utter bitch. To be completely honest, I kind of was. I didn't have friends; I had minions and wannabes that followed me around like lost puppies. I was the girl that every boy wanted, and every girl wanted to be. The socialite constantly stalked by paparazzi with a slew of hookups in her wake. The trendsetter, the beauty queen, the diva.

I was everything but myself.

It was almost as if I was a player in a video game, but I was being controlled by a monkey on acid. I ran into walls, tripped over air, and ninety-nine percent of the time looked completely lost and oblivious. I often wondered if my life was just a big joke and God and the angels sat up in heaven laughing at me.

Ha. Ha. Ha. Look at this mistake. You see? This is what a human shouldn't be.

It was *super* empowering.

"How is everything tasting?" Asher reappeared at our table, breaking me from my depressing reverie. His eyes flickered briefly over the other occupants before coming to rest on me. He offered me a crooked smile.

"It's delicious, thank you," I responded, chasing down a bite of my alfredo with a cup of water.

"It's acceptable. The meat's a little dry, however. I would like to speak to the cook about that." D.O.D.'s eyes narrowed. Of course, my dad couldn't go one freaking minute without acting like a complete asshole. And you wonder why I have no friends?

Asher visibly stiffened, but he managed another serene smile.

"Of course. I'll go get him for you right away."

I wanted to tell him that it wasn't necessary, that I understood the restaurant was packed and taking away the head chef in the middle of the dinner-rush was beyond idiotic, but I kept my mouth shut. I tried to convey with my eyes how sorry I was for, well, everything.

Something in my expression must've distracted him, because one second he was staring at me, and the next he was lurching forward. The plate of food he was carrying shattered on the floor, food flying through the air to land in Buttlicker's lap. Dickhead immediately jumped to his feet, surveying Asher as if he was a potential threat.

I felt my body grow cold.

It was obviously an accident, but I knew my father and

the people he surrounded himself with. The best-case scenario would be the waiter getting a good old firing. The worst...

Thinking quickly, I threw back my head and let out a lilting laugh. Every eye at the table immediately turned to stare at me. The usual chatter in the restaurant diminished around us until all I could hear was Asher's pounding heart as he picked himself up behind me.

D.O.D. pinched the bridge of his nose.

"What the hell are you laughing at?"

I smoothed my expression into one of icy impassiveness. I called it my bitch face, one that I reserved only for meetings like these. It was a part that I had long since perfected. Bitch me was almost like an extension of my hand.

"I didn't appreciate the way the waiter was ogling me," I said flippantly, scowling at Asher. He blinked at me, momentarily speechless. "So, I taught him a little lesson about respect." I tossed my hair over my shoulder for effect. I had seen girls do it in movies, so I figured why the hell not?

You got this, Adelaide. You're a bad bitch.

D.O.D.'s hands tightened around his cup until I could see his blue veins protruding from his alabaster skin.

"You tripped him."

It wasn't a question.

"I just wanted to teach him some respect, daddy dearest. Isn't that what you always told me?" Yeah, so maybe now I was being a sarcastic bitch instead of just a mean bitch, but I couldn't help it. He always seemed to bring out the worst in me. Maybe I just figured that whatever punishment he dished out wouldn't change no matter how bad I was. I could murder someone, and it would be just as bad as if I were to cuss at the dinner table.

Not as if I had ever murdered someone before, mind you.

For a moment I thought he was going to yell at me in

front of the entire restaurant. I even feared that he would throw his cup at me. Glass was a pain to get out of my skin and hair. After what felt like an eternity, he released a breath while simultaneously releasing the cup. I felt like I could breathe again.

"We will discuss this tonight," he said stoutly, turning back towards his meal. His eyes promised pain. Lots and lots of pain. Buttlicker, beside me, grinned like the deviant I knew him to be.

"If you don't mind me asking, Sir, but I would be more than willing help you administer punishment."

My fork clattered against my plate, and my mouth dropped open.

God no. Please no. Not again. No. No. No.

"I believe we could come to an agreement," D.O.D. said with a tiny smile. "If you, of course, agree to my original proposition."

Once again, the conversation turned back towards buildings and real-estate and all that other fun stuff. I, however, felt as if I couldn't breathe. My body felt cold, as if someone had dumped a bucket of ice over my head. It was a numb type of cold. Painful, almost, but dulling as the seconds dragged on.

I noticed that Asher hadn't moved from where he stood behind me, food covering his white shirt. Nobody paid him any mind as the conversation veered towards contracts – not even my mother was staring at him any longer – but I could feel his eyes caressing my back. I tried my hardest to ignore him, tried my hardest to face forward, but the urge to turn around was almost unbearable. Finally, I couldn't resist any longer.

His eyes were anguished when they met mine. His thick, ebony lashes feathered against his cheekbones. Just as suddenly, the expression was swept away by a tidal wave of anger. His gaze turned towards my father, who seemed utterly oblivious to the penetrating gaze searing his skin.

I recognized that look. It was the same look I have both given and received. That look promised pain and revenge.

It was also a look that made me, almost innately, hopeful.

CHAPTER 2

*a*spen Resort was an immense structure located in the dead center of nowhere. Only the surrounding trees rivaled the log structure, their coniferous needles coated with a soft layer of fluffy snow. Besides the trees, occasionally splintering off to create a small enclosure for ice ranks and hills for skiing, the town of Aspen was devoid of anything that remotely resembled a normal city. There was no theater, no restaurant, no mall. Of course, there was no need for any of that. Not with Aspen Resort.

I was all too familiar with the commodities that came with the tourist trap. It drew you in like a fly to a spider web, entangling you until you became stuck. And no, I am not being dramatic.

I really hated Aspen Resort, my home for the better part of my seventeen years.

There might've been a time, when I was an infant, where I lived a semi-normal life. I have a vague recollection of a petite house nestled in a suburban neighborhood. Of course, that could all just be a wistful fantasy I had constructed from the various books I read and television shows I watched.

I only found one spot peaceful in all of Aspen Resort. It was a relatively small room when compared to the rest of the building, but it was my own. The diminutive poolroom was usually abandoned. A couple of years ago, my parents decided to create an indoor water park and an Olympic size pool near the lobby of the resort. That left the old pool – which I coined the wannabe beach – all by its lonesome, a considerable distance away from the rest of the amenities the resort had to offer.

The wannabe beach consisted of nothing more than a few tables, ornamented with colorful umbrellas, and a makeshift plastic sun in the far corner of the room. The walls were painted with what were supposed to be palm trees but were beginning to fade away from years of neglect. I was honestly surprised my parents still allowed this room to exist in their perfect resort. I assumed they forgot about it, just as they often forgot about their daughter.

I pulled my brown hair up into a disheveled bun. Surveying myself in the mirror, I bit my lip. When had I gotten so skinny? Even in my one-piece bathing suit, a stylish, black number with silver adorning the top, I could see the curves of my hips. The thought should've worried me. Once upon a time, it *would've* worried me. Now, all I felt was…empty.

There was no other word to describe it.

My gaze flickered to my arms, visible with my bathing suit. There was no way I could go to the pool like that, even if it was empty. The halls were always bustling with people. Sighing, I reached for my coverup inside my dresser. Long-sleeved, of course, and falling just above my knee.

My father would reprimand me for wearing such an outfit.

"A whore!" he would announce. "You shouldn't be showing so much leg."

My mother, on the other hand, would look me over with a critical eye and demand that I show more of my body.

"It's important for business, sweetheart." It was always the same tone with her. Haughty and imperious, with a set to her chin that came from years and years of power. The type of tone that made me squirm just thinking about it.

Letting out an exasperated grunt, I grabbed my book off my chair and tip-toed out of my room. I needed to be careful that I didn't alert anyone to my presence – from my parents, to the guards, to Mr. Buttlicker that I just knew I'd find lurking somewhere near my bedroom. It wouldn't be the first time that my parents handed out such information, and it definitely wouldn't be the last.

Finding the hall empty, I stealthily crept towards the elevator, sighing with content when the light dinged. The wannabe beach was at the ground level, below even the lobby. It felt like years until the doors finally slid open.

Walking briskly past the occasional straggler – though what idiot would be up at this time of night? Wait. Me. *I'm* the idiot. – I moved to the door at the end of the hallway. I was always wary about swimming laps, even when I knew the area remained abandoned most of the time. If one person was to walk in and see me...

If one person was to see my arms...

Boisterous laughter interrupted my musings. Frowning, I pushed open the door...to see the pool swarming with teenagers.

Those filthy sons of bitches...

I gritted my teeth together and resisted the urge to throw my book at the nearest person. I was really, really, *really* not a people person. And I was really, really, *really* looking forward to some time by myself.

Maybe if I shitted in the pool...?

My mind ran through all the possibilities.

Oh God. I was officially losing my mind. Soon, I would be huddled in a bunker muttering about the old woman that dared speak to me in the grocery store.

I debated whether I wanted to escape back to my room. The option was not tempting. Knowing my luck, and my parents, I'd find Buttlicker waiting for me. I trembled with revulsion at the thought.

No, I would much rather take my chances with drunk teenagers than old perverts.

Spotting an empty chair in the corner, I hurried to sit down. I learned long ago how to ignore everyone around me. To drift away, to empty myself so I would feel nothing at all. It wasn't the safest coping mechanism, but it got me through the day.

Sort of.

I turned blindly to a page in my book, my attention momentarily fixed on the scene before me. I wondered if a school group was here. Usually we only got old farts, rich families, or the occasional teenager coming up for their school break. Never this many, and never ones that seemed to all know each other.

Girls and guys were making out in the pool. A group was playing a game of water volleyball. Chicken fighting over in the shallow end. A game of spin-the-bottle.

Two girls stepped in front of me, their attention as fixated on the pool as mine was. The two blondes wore the skimpiest bikinis imaginable. Seriously, the poor fabric looked as if it was straining against their considerable chests. I was not lacking in the chest department by any means, but those two girls put mine to shame. I scoffed.

They were too round and perfect to be real.

What type of high schooler was allowed to get a breast job? What type of parents would allow that?

I thought of my mother and her condescending smile.

Ugh, that smirk. I hated that smirk. I wanted to punch that smirk off her face. She would most definitely be okay with me getting a breast job. Anything to help the family business.

"Do you see Ryder?" The blond in the pink bikini asked, flicking her hair over her shoulder.

"Don't worry, Missy. He'll come," Purple reassured her friend. Pink – Missy, I assumed – glowered.

"He's probably off with Declan or something," Missy finally conceded, though she didn't sound convinced. They stayed silent for a moment, each one surveying the pool with predatory glints in their eyes.

"Do you think I look okay?" Purple asked suddenly, twisting to show off her purple bikini, the cause of her namesake.

"You look fine," Missy snapped. "And if you don't think you look good, change bikinis."

"But I only brought one bikini."

Missy's mouth dropped open. "Are you serious? I brought like three. But you're not a cheerleader so you wouldn't understand."

Huh? I raised an eyebrow, thoroughly intrigued. This was ten times better than my book.

"But I do dance," Purple insisted.

What the actual fuck was happening?

"You only brought one," Missy sighed. She looked honestly upset by that prospect. Still sulking, she turned and walked towards the water volleyball game. Purple followed her like an obedient puppy.

"Oh my gosh, did you hear that? She only brought *one* bikini?" The voice came from beside me, making me startle. I turned with almost blistering speed and nearly fell off my chair when I met the laughing eyes of the person beside me.

Oh, sweet Jesus have mercy…

He was hot. Like sex-on-a-stick hot. Bronzed skin, amber eyes, tousled black hair with green highlights at the tips. And his body. It was a work of art. It would take me hours to fully appreciate every detail depicted across his abs, every intricately designed vine and flower and…was that a unicorn? Somehow, that mythical creature etched into his skin demoted him from intimidating to approachable. I mean, seriously, any guy willing to flaunt a unicorn must have serious balls.

Don't think about his balls, Adelaide. Don't think about his... dammit now I'm thinking about them.

"I can't believe it," Sexy continued on, his voice rising a few octaves as he attempted to adopt a valley-girl accent.

I pitched my voice in a similar fashion to his. "I know, right? I brought, like, eight. One for dipping my toes in…"

"One for sitting at the pool in," he continued, fighting a grin.

"One for going waist deep. Only waist deep. And of course, I have one entirely made of satin." I dramatically flipped my hair over my shoulder to emphasize my point.

He looked at me in mock horror. "Only one?"

"I mean, you wouldn't understand. I have, like, hobbies and interests and stuff."

"And activities?"

"Oh my god, who does activities? Seriously?"

A laugh escaped his lips.

"What's your name, doll?" he asked, his voice dropping back to what I assumed was his normal tone.

Oh, and what a fine voice he has...

"I have a fine voice?" Sexy asked, raising a pierced eyebrow in my direction.

"Oh shit. I said that aloud, didn't I?" I questioned, not at all perturbed. You get used to it after a while. The amount of times I had said stupid stuff…well…it's no wonder I have no friends and my parents hated me.

"I just don't have a filter, I guess. But I mean you *do* have a nice voice. It's all husky and sultry and stuff. You'd probably be a good singer." I was rambling, my go-to move when confronted with cute guys.

Sexy stared at me a moment before bursting into laughter.

"I would love to hear you say that in front of Ryder," he remarked. Before I could inquire, he turned towards me. "So, am I going to get a name?"

Shrugging, I pointed towards the ditzy blond in the skimpy bikini I had seen earlier.

"I heard her name is Missy."

"Well, my name is Ronan." He extended a hand, and I shook it after a slight hesitation.

"Nice to meet you, Ronan with the satin bikinis."

He smirked. "And the fine voice."

"How could I forget?"

Shifting in my seat, I turned back towards my forgotten book, effectively ending the conversation.

"I haven't seen you around. You don't go to Highwood Prep?"

I guess I *wasn't* effectively ending the conversation. Looking down the bridge of my nose, this time, I smirked at him.

"How do you know?"

"Because I would've remembered someone like you." He gave me an appreciatory stare that made goosebumps break out across my skin.

"Maybe I was just hiding. From you."

Shrugging, I sprawled myself out in my seat and turned the page on my book. I felt him, almost as if he was charged with electricity, come up beside me.

"So, are you here on vacation?"

I hesitated, only briefly, before nodding.

"Yes."

I mean, what else could I do? Tell him that my parents owned the damned place? What a good conversation starter: "My parents are members of the mafia, and you're staying at their shady-ass, illegal business and talking to their daughter."

Ha.

Of course, most people didn't know that my parents were not, well, *normal* business entrepreneurs. But I knew.

"Are you going to go into the pool?" Ronan asked.

"Oh, that just sounds dandy," I drawled. I held up my book. "Because obviously I'm not in the middle of doing anything. Now shut up and leave me alone. I'm at a good part."

His silence lasted for approximately fifteen seconds.

"What'cha reading?"

"Oh for the love of..." Before I could stop myself, I wacked him on the head with the book. It didn't hurt him because I was a weakling, but his eyes widened in shock.

"Did you just hit me with your book?"

"I told you, I'm at a good part," I pointed out, biting my lip to keep from smirking. Believe it or not, I liked talking to Ronan. He was one of the least douchiest people I have met at Aspen Resort so far. It was always fun to flirt with the tourists.

I knew I was beautiful. Hell, I doubt my parents would keep me around if I wasn't. My beauty served as both my shield and my sword. My defense and my offense. Today, I was on the hunt. Not that I would let anything happen between the tourist and me, of course. I couldn't afford to let them get close, and I *definitely* didn't want them facing my parent's wrath.

But it was nice to pretend.

"You are a strange girl," Ronan said, but he did so with a smile. I kept my attention fixated on my book as I turned a page.

"Still at a good part."

"Ronan! Baby!" A shrill, feminine voice cooed.

I set the book on my lap, pinching the bridge of my nose.

"I swear to God, Ronan, you have exactly five seconds to get rid of that voice before I castrate you."

Ronan nearly fell out of his seat from laughing so hard. I should've felt guilty – after all, I had just insulted a total stranger who obviously knew Ronan – but that voice was annoying. How did anyone listen to that…sound?

The girl that stepped up was beautiful. There was no other word to describe her. If Ronan was sexy and danger-ous, this girl was flowers and cupcakes. A dewy face with emerald eyes, framed by thick lashes and auburn hair that cascaded down her back. An hourglass figure. I supposed she had to be beautiful to have a voice like that.

"Who's your little…friend?" Her eyes ran over me, the malice in them nearly smoldering.

I take back my early assessment. She was most definitely not flowers and cupcakes. If anything, she was wilted flowers and poisoned cupcakes.

"Elena," Ronan said stiffly. His body was taut.

"I was looking for you," Elena hissed. That voice…I shuddered.

To Ronan, I mumbled, "Five seconds."

"Five seconds until what?" huffed Elena, her penetrating gaze swiveling my way. I resisted the urge to stick my tongue out at her like a child. Or give her the finger like an adult. Either option appealed to me, honestly. Maybe I could do a combination…?

A smile ghosted across Ronan's lips before it contorted into a cold mask.

"I'll meet you by the entryway, Elena," he said evenly.

"But-"

"The entryway or not at all."

It was a contest of wills, his dark eyes locked with her vibrant green ones. The air around them practically seemed to spark with electricity. Elena broke away first, scowling, before storming towards the door of the poolroom. She did not look pleased.

"Well, damn," I stated. "That was intense. I *felt* the tension. Or was that sexual tension? Hmm…I guess the world may never know. Actually, that's not true. If you guys start pawing at each other, then it was most definitely sexual tension."

Ronan stared at me with an unreadable expression.

"Trust me. That was the exact opposite of sexual tension."

"So it was platonic tension, then?" I pressed. When he didn't respond, I shrugged nonchalantly. "Dude, I feel ya. Platonic tension is intense. It makes you lose control. Like, you suddenly want a hug from your brother or something."

"What is wrong with you?" The question did not hold any malice. If anything, he sounded bemused, as if I was a puzzle he was struggling to solve. I considered his question thoughtfully before responding,

"A lot actually."

Sighing, I scooped up my book and folded my towel. I suppose I could always read in my room behind a locked door.

"Wait! Where are you going?" Ronan seemed confused.

I patted his cheek. "I told you already. I'm hiding from you."

Maybe I was slightly insane. Maybe I wasn't. At that moment, I didn't care. The way he looked at me made me feel as if I was the most beautiful girl to have existed.

Not sexy, but as if I was someone cherished. No one had ever looked at me like that. With awe.

"I never caught your name!" Ronan shouted after me. He sat rooted to the spot next to our chairs, hands outstretched as if he could pull me back to him.

"That's because I never gave you anything to catch!" I called back.

CHAPTER 3

*G*iselle was muttering again.

She had two, distinct types of mutterings. One I would often refer to as her annoyed mutters. They would be nearly inarticulate phrases hissed beneath her breath and accompanied by a small shake of her head. My least favorite, and the most frequent, were her pissed off mutterings. These would involve a lot of swear words and a lot of random statements sewn together. Once, I believed I heard her make up a pretty interesting curse concerning a monkey, a lawnmower, and plastic surgery, but I could never be certain. With the latter utterances, her face turned beet red, and her eyes narrowed into slits. She had always been a condescending woman, but with her eyes probing my scalp as if she could physically skin me alive, she became terrifying.

Fortunately for me, I had grown immune.

"Can't you do anything?" she snapped. The question was vague, though I suspected it was because she didn't expect an answer. Still, being the smartass I was, I made a show of considering her words.

"I can recite the alphabet backwards," I said innocently. I held the coffee cup up to my lips and took a tentative sip. It was still scorching hot, but the cream helped damper the heat. I was always a bear if I didn't have approximately five hundred cups in the morning. Hell, I was a bear even *with* my coffee.

"I can also hold my pee in until the very last possible second," I continued, watching her face pinch together. "Let me see…Oh! I can put my toe in my ear. And I definitely have a talent with fire. On my last birthday alone, I lit my hair on fire…though I don't think that really counts as my fault. It totally was the candle's."

Giselle shot me a glare that could've withered grapes into raisins. If I could only use one word to describe my tutor, it would be mousey. Of course, she would probably whoop my ass if she ever heard me describe her as such, but the older woman just reminded me of a petite mouse. She kept her gray hair cut short around her small, elfin face. Her body was wiry, nothing more than bones and wrinkled skin.

Still, Mrs. Baldwin was a scary son-of-a-gun.

"I don't even know why we do these lessons anyway," I said, when it became apparent that she wasn't going to respond. Moving from my seat at the counter, I poured myself another cup of coffee. A girl needed at least twenty in an hour if she didn't want to become a murderer. "I already graduated high school and college. This is stupid and overkill."

I graduated high school when I was only thirteen, courtesy of Mrs. Giselle Baldwin herself. Online college followed immediately after. Heaven forbid that my parents let me attend public school…like Highwood Prep. Not that I wanted to go there or anything. Nope. Not me. Who needed social interaction with kids her own age? Not this girl. Nope.

Nada. Who needed social interaction with kids her own age or boys with unicorn tattoos across their chests? Definitely not me.

Giselle still didn't answer me, possibly too angry to speak.

With a roll of my eyes, I turned back towards the textbook she had laid out in front of me. Business Law and Relevant Cases. *Oh joy*. Because there was nothing else I would rather do than study business law cases.

"Are we done with lessons for today?" I asked in my sweetest tone, batting my eyelashes for effect.

We were in my suite, an immense, multi-room space located on the upper floor of the resort, entirely separate from my parents'. We currently sat inside the kitchen, which was nothing more than an open space with sleek, marble flooring and a wide, granite countertop. Off the right wall was my small dining room, though I barely used it. Why would I want to sit at a dining room table by myself? Even for me, a girl that talked to herself, *that* was entirely too depressing.

The living room was just as extravagant as the rest of the place: a leather, black sofa, a television mounted to the wall, and a collection of armchairs arranged into a makeshift circle.

Overall, the place was devoid of any personalization. If it wasn't for the scattering of clothes in my bedroom, some might wonder if the suite was even occupied. I may be living here, but it sure as hell wasn't my home. It felt too cold, too empty, too lonely.

Despite feeling this way, the idea of moving in with my parents made my skin crawl. I was stuck in perpetual isolation. I could be around hundreds of people, yet my heart still ached as if it was just me. Maybe it was because nobody ever saw *me*. Sure, they saw the beautiful girl that my parents desired me to be, but nobody looked past such a superficial mask. Did they see my scars, both mental and physical? Did they understand that my sarcasm and wit were a defense mechanism?

Did they understand I was barely hanging on?

My hand, went to my arm covered by my red sweater. Sunlight trickled through the kitchen window in soft beams, making the temperature in the kitchen stifling. Still, I knew I couldn't take off my sweater. Not with Giselle around.

Not ever.

"I suppose we can stop for now. Despite your obvious attention problems, you are far enough ahead that we can call it a day." Though her mouth was set into a thin line, her eyes warmed slightly. Giselle loved to brag about her teaching skills, but I would've been fine just learning the material myself.

I found it all easy.

I couldn't tell you how to change a tire, but if you asked me to configure data for a property, I'm your girl.

Taking another sip of my coffee, I opened my mouth to thank Giselle for my few hours of free time – I had to meet D.O.D. in a couple hours for a meeting – when something on the television caught my attention. Frowning, I hurried past my aging tutor and into the living room. The remote was where I left it, smothered between two couch cushions (totally intentional), and I quickly turned the volume up.

"…so far, only five casualties have been reported, though this may increase over time."

The footage switched away from the newscaster to what once might've been a pretty town but was now nothing more than piles of debris and broken homes. Everything was in shambles; I couldn't discern one house from the next.

Frowning, I squinted my eyes at the screen to make sure I'd read the heading correctly.

FOUR TORNADOS HIT BRACKEN, ALASKA

Alaska? Tornados? That was a rare phenomenon all on its own, but four?

The footage switched once again. The camera shook – obviously the work of an amateur – but it still managed to capture the moment the tornado touched down, a swirling sheet of dirt and debris. The camera panned away, and almost instantly, another tornado appeared a little bit away from the first. They seemed to dance around one another, tilting towards each other like forbidden lovers but never once touching. It happened a third time. And a fourth time.

The trees folded underneath the intensity of the winds; the houses, before my very eyes, began to collapse in on themselves, like old, yellowing paper. The newscaster was speaking, but I couldn't hear over the roaring in my ears.

How awful...

"I agree. It is awful." I hadn't even realized that Giselle had come in behind me. I also hadn't realized that I had spoken aloud – not that I was surprised, mind you. "Your family has property up there. I hope there weren't any damages"

My hands fisted against my sides.

"That's what you're worried about?" I asked, barely able to reign in my temper. "One of our *many* properties? What about the houses that have been destroyed? The lives that have been lost?"

Giselle tilted her head to the side, silver hair appearing almost like starlight in the artificial lighting. I had never considered my tutor cruel before. Mean, yes. A hard-ass, most definitely. But cruel? Evil?

Just now, though, she was looking at me as if *I* was the mistake. As if *I* had an issue.

When she spoke, her voice was uncharacteristically kind. "My dear, I prepared you so much better than this. There is no them. There is only you and us. Why be shoved when you can shove? Why be dead when you can kill? Why care when you're better than them?"

I resisted the urge to roll my eyes. That was Giselle for you. Always spewing wisdom. And you wonder why I'm a little fucked up?

∼

I SAW him a moment before he saw me.

How could I not notice him? He looked just as gorgeous as he was the first time I saw him. His blond hair was lightly tousled as if he had run his hand through it one too many times. His body was lithe and defined, muscles accentuated in the faded t-shirt he wore and blue jeans. His eyes brightened when he saw me as if someone had lit a candle beneath the surface.

"I know you!" he said, walking forward. Sure, he was attractive, but I had met a lot of attractive guys in my life. He was just another pretty face in a sea of, well, pretty faces.

I feigned impassiveness as I considered him coolly.

"The waiter, correct? Ashton?"

"Asher," he corrected. He remained silent for a minute, a blush staining his cheeks. "So, what are you up to?"

"Last I checked I was walking down the hallway," I said dryly. "But I'm stopped now, so I suppose you could say I'm standing in the hallway."

His blush deepened, and he opened his mouth to speak, shut it, and then opened it again. He looked like a gaping fish. An adorable, blond fish, but a fish all the same.

I decided to have pity on the poor, unfortunate soul.

"I was actually going to the wanna...I mean the pool. To read." I held up my book. "I didn't get a lot of reading done yesterday." The final statement came out as an annoyed grumble. Asher cracked a smile at that.

"Somebody annoyed you?" he guessed, sounding amused. I scowled.

"You could say that."

"Well, I just wanted to thank you for what you did the other night. Sticking up for me, I mean. Taking the fall so I wouldn't get fired." He let out a sigh, his hand running through his blond locks.

"It's fine," I said quickly, hoping he'd drop the subject. The last thing I wanted to do was discuss emotions and feelings and all that shit. I shuddered just thinking about it.

"Well, it was a pretty cool thing for you to do."

"Yup."

"And I just wanted to say thank you."

"Okay."

I was not the most eloquent speaker, was I? Asher shuffled from one foot to the next. Judging from his scuffling and shifty eyes, he wanted to say something else to me, something important. But I needed to tell him something too.

I'd never warned anyone before. Did it make me a horrible person that I knew all this information, yet I kept it to myself like a good girl? Did it make me a coward?

I don't know why I told Asher what I did. Maybe it was the way he looked at me, his eyes the bluest of blues. Maybe the vulnerability and tenderness on his face made me do it. Or maybe, and this was probably the more likely explanation, I was just a sucker for attractive guys.

"Look, Asher, if you want my advice…quit your job. You're young, good-looking, and probably smarter than half of the people hired at this resort. Find a job modeling or something. Just don't work here. Ever." Asher's eyes widened at my assertion. He opened his mouth as if to ask me why I would say such a crude thing when I cut him off. Again. "Now why don't you run along and listen to a chilling rendition of Celine Dion's *My Heart Will Go On*, or whatever it is you boys do now a day." He continued to stare at me as if I had suddenly sprouted a second head.

Gah. This was why I didn't talk to boys. They annoyed me.

"Chop. Chop." I clapped my hands for emphasis. "Run along, Goldilocks. Go find yourself some porridge."

Still nothing. Not even a twitch this time.

"Sacrifice ravens and stain the trees with their blood?"

I got a mere blink. The transformation from a prowling, flirtatious tiger to this shell-shocked boy terrified me a bit. And provided a touch of entertainment, if I was so inclined to admit such a thing to myself.

"Play jump rope dressed as Humpty Dumpty? Belly dance around a volcano? No? Does none of that sound interesting to you?"

How difficult was it to please this man? Geez.

"I…" He finally said. I watched his Adam's apple bob as he swallowed. "I wanted to invite you to breakfast with me and some of my friends. As a thank you."

My stomach growled at the mere mention of breakfast. Daddy insisted that I ration what I ate (read as: eat literally nothing in order to keep my figure minus a few business-oriented dinners).

"Will there be coffee?" I demanded, raising an eyebrow. I had to get the important questions out of the way.

He still seemed stunned, maybe even scared. Who could blame him? I *was* a little crazy. Okay, maybe a lot of crazy.

"Yes?" The statement turned into a shaky question.

"Then why are we still standing here? Coffee awaits, my gentle knight."

Linking my arm through his, I practically dragged him down the hall. It was only when we arrived at the lobby did Asher come back to his senses.

"Um…we're going the wrong way."

"Right. Of course. I knew that."

I dragged him down another hallway.

"Still the wrong way."

I stomped my foot into the ground and pouted. Why was it so difficult for a woman to get her coffee?

I kept the game up for a few more minutes – opening up a random door, feigning obliviousness, and leading a very amused Asher to another section of the resort.

"Okay. Okay," Asher huffed after I dragged him towards a supply closet. "I'm too lazy to do all this walking. And I'm hungry. Exercise and hunger did not make a great combination for a growing boy."

At the first statement, I gave him a pointed once-over. The boy was fit, to put it bluntly, and could've easily ran around the entire resort numerous times. It was *my* lazy, frail ass that was beginning to pant erratically. Okay, so maybe not my ass (because asses can't pant), but you get what I meant.

"Fine," I obliged, tugging on his jacket sleeve. "Let's go little Ms. Waiter."

"Ms.?" he asked, eyebrow raised. I shrugged.

"You have very feminine, pretty features." When he continued to stare at me, I added, "And you sort of remind me of a girl PMSing. You know, the whole food thing."

He tilted his head to the side. I may have considered his expression thoughtful if not for the wicked glint in his eye.

"I can't say I have ever been compared to a female before." He didn't sound at all offended, only amused. "I can assure you that I am all man, sweetie."

"Laying it on thick, Ash?" a voice, booming with laughter, asked. "That was the most pathetic, ball-clenching pickup line I had ever heard before."

Asher's face turned a dark red as he faced the newcomer above my shoulder.

Well that was just rude.

Twinkling out a laugh a couple octaves higher than my normal voice – channeling my inner Elena (the bimbo from the pool) – I placed my hand on Asher's bicep.

"Oh, Ashy! You have such a way with words." Another laugh.

It was so annoying I almost wanted to slap myself.

"You totally know how to win over a woman." I took a strand of my hair and curled it around my finger. Lowering my voice, I added, "And if last night was any indication, please a woman as well."

If it was possible – and I didn't think it physically was – Asher's face went five shades redder. With a wink, I braced myself, turning to face the intruder that dared insult Asher.

Okay, so maybe I came across as a territorial bitch, but Asher was the only semi-decent guy I have met, and it was a shame that he felt embarrassed. Not that it wasn't cute or anything to see red blotches on his cheeks…

Nope. Nada. Totally hideous and not at all sexy to see a gorgeous man blush.

My breath let my body in one big whoosh when I faced the newcomer. Was every boy in this resort drop-dead, mouth-wateringly beautiful?

The new guy was gorgeous; there was no other way to describe it. While Asher sported more standard, boy-next-door good looks, this new one screamed danger. A sexy sort of danger, but danger all the same.

He had strong, broad shoulders, clearly noticeable in his black-fitted tee. His defined cheekbones appeared chiseled, and his hair was cropped close to his head. His dark skin showcased several tattoos – not as many as Ronan had, but enough to keep me intrigued. It was his eyes, though, that captured my attention. They were almost an amber color, bright and smoldering in an already arresting face.

Every fiber of my being wanted to fan myself like a blushing schoolgirl. It took incredible restraint on my part to keep my face impassive. Honestly, I was pretty proud of myself. If they handed out gold medals in the Olympics for resisting handsome boys, then I would receive them all. Gold medals, that is, not the boys. Okay, maybe some of the boys.

Focus, Adelaide. And stop drooling.

The new boy smirked, and I realized I had said that thought aloud. Oh well. You can't win them all, can you?

"And who might you be?" I gave him a dismissive once-over as if he was nothing but a pesky bug. I'm sure that he could see through my apathetic front (hell, he would have to be an idiot not to), but he didn't call me out on it. I appreciated his respect in allowing me to ogle him without admonishment

"The name is Ryder," he said, grabbing my hand and pressing a kiss to the skin there. Yup. He most definitely saw through my less-than-impressed attitude...or he was just a cocky bastard. I chose to believe it was the latter.

But his lips though...

I barely resisted the urge to roll my eyes. He went from sexy to cheesy in a span of five seconds. With a wicked smile, he kept a firm grip on my hand. I wanted to accidentally (but very purposefully) knee him in the balls.

"And what might your name be?" he continued. "Probably a beautiful name for a beautiful girl?"

I couldn't help it. A laugh bubbled up from my chest before I could stop myself.

"Oh my god. That is so fucking corny. Does that actually work for you? Good grief, I need a shower now to replace the stench of shitty pickup lines." I giggled at Ryder's blank expression and slowly extracted my hand. The traitorous limb still tingled from his kiss. "Now run along and head back to your computer so you can look up better pickup lines. Go on. *Shoo*." I waved him away with a flick of my wrist.

Ryder was silent for only a moment, before he said, playing off of my word shoo, "Flipflop." Pause. "Croc."

I shook my head. "See? So freaking corny." A smile betrayed my amusement. "You remind me of a cat – constantly rubbing against everyone for pleasure."

"That's nicer than what she said to me," Asher interjected. "She called me feminine."

Ryder erupted into laughter. He practically fell over.

Good. I hope you choke on your laughter...that is, if you can choke on laughter. I meant your spit. Choke on your spit, you cocky son of a-

My inner monologue (which somehow became my outer monologue) only made Ryder laugh harder. Tears formed in his eyes, and he hastily brushed them away.

"I can't say that I disagree with her assessment," Ryder said after he collected himself. "I meant the part about you being feminine, not me choking on my laughter." He side-stepped the hit Asher aimed at his head.

Turning towards me, Ryder rewarded me with an indolent smirk. He really did remind me of a cat: a lazy, sprawling cat that expected the world to drop at its feet as nothing more than filthy peasants.

"But seriously, what's your name, Kitten?"

Snorting at the nickname, I ignored him and turned back towards Asher.

"So, are we heading to get food and coffee or not? You can't promise a girl food and renege – I have castrated boys for a lot less."

"Wait?" Ryder interrupted. "She's joining us for lunch?"

I frowned. "Wait? He's joining us for lunch?"

"You can't just copy me!"

"You can't just copy me," I mocked, lowering my voice to match Ryder's husky tone. I admit that I took a few creative liberties in my impression of him.

"Stop it."

"Stop it."

"Seriously, Kitten."

"Seriously, Kitten."

"Stop-"

"Will you stop acting like a child, Ryder?" Asher exclaimed, sounding exasperated. Ryder opened his mouth and then closed it soundlessly. He pointed to me like a reprimanded schoolboy passing the blame.

I decided that I liked Asher a little bit more.

Poking Ryder in the ribs, I smirked at him. "Come on *child*, let's go get food."

I hurried ahead of them before he could retort. As I turned the corner, I heard Ryder mutter something about "favoritism" and "breasts". Oh well. Mama can't help what she was born with.

WE WENT to a small café on the outskirts of the resort. Styled after a 70's red-seated diner, Rosie's House failed to mimic the opulence displayed elsewhere in the resort. I was honestly surprised that D.O.D. allowed such a normal place to exist in his "prestigious establishment" (his words).

I personally liked Rosie's House, despite no one named Rosie actually working there. Maybe it was because my dad hated it. Maybe I went only as a big middle finger towards D.O.D. and Mommy Dearest.

I recognized the hostess as a young woman named Shannon. She spotted us immediately and batted her lashes at the two boys. Ryder straightened his spine. He was a lion that wasn't just out for the hunt, but for the kill.

He leaned against the host podium, smile sly. "And what might your name be? Probably a beautiful name for a beautiful girl."

I snorted, turning my face towards Asher to conceal my laughter.

The poor boy needed help. His skills were severely lacking. Fortunately for him, I had been told I was a great wingman (wingwoman?).

Schooling my features, I turned back towards Shannon and Ryder, the former of which was giggling and kicking her foot.

"So Ryder was telling me about his modeling gig," I said cheerfully. Both Ryder's and Asher's eyebrows rose. I just winked. Something akin to understanding flickered across Ryder's features.

"Well, I don't want to brag…" he drawled, trying to act sheepish. I snorted yet again. Ryder didn't seem to have a modest bone in his body. Yes, he was attractive, but did he have to let the entire world know that he knew? Okay, so maybe I was biased (because, for some reason, Ryder just seemed to piss me off), but he could've at least had *some* class.

I decided to up the ante, so to speak. Giving a shit-eating grin, I continued, "And tell her about your offer. Pro-football? What was the team again?" I batted my eyelashes, feigning ignorance. Behind me, Asher burst into laughter, though he quickly tried to mask it into a cough.

"I…um…" I imagined this was one of the few times that the great Ryder got flustered.

"You play football?" Shannon asked dreamily. "I only ever date football players."

Yuck. Gag. Ew.

A "hump me now" sign would've come off less desperate.

"Well, unfortunately for you, I'm not interested," Ryder said briskly. I gaped at him. His sudden change in behavior was surprising, to put it mildly.

Shannon seemed just as stunned, if not slightly pissed. Without another word, she spun on her heel and hurried in the direction of the kitchen.

I guess we weren't going to get seated after all.

Huffing with indignation, I put my hands on my hips.

"What the hell was that about? You are a horrible flirt."

Ryder shrugged, a beautiful grin touching his gorgeous face.

"She only dates football players." Tilting his head towards mine, so his breath caressed my cheek, he murmured, "I'm a musician."

"You're also an ungrateful swine. I totally could've gotten you laid. Never ask me to be your wingman again!"

He straightened. "I never asked you the first time," he pointed out. That stupid grin still graced his face.

"It was a gift! You...you...ass!" I sputtered in mock outrage, but inside I was having fun. Talking to these boys, joking with them, helped me forget everything else transpiring daily in my miserable excuse of a life. So sue me, but I actually liked the cocky bastard. He kept me entertained.

"Now come on, Casanova," Asher said. "I'm hungry and the others are probably getting impatient."

Ryder muttered under his breath yet again (I wondered if he even realized he was doing it or if he was like me) before he obediently followed Asher.

"Ha," I whispered, swindling up beside him. "So whipped." He shoved at my shoulder, and I shoved back. He, of course, only shoved me harder.

"Seriously? You can't go around hitting girls." Asher sounded moderately horrified. Ryder gave a small shrug.

"She started it."

Something Asher said previously struck me like a bolt of lightning all of a sudden. I froze mid-step, barely registering when Ryder ran into my back.

"Wait. Others? There's more of you?" I wanted to add that two hot boys were enough but didn't want to risk inflating Ryder's already immense ego.

"Yeah," Asher said absently, leading us to a large booth in the back. "We're here on a school trip."

"What type of school takes a field trip to a resort?" I questioned, bemused.

"Ours, *obviously*," Ryder huffed. I was tempted to stick my tongue out at him. Instead of physical sarcasm, I settled for verbal.

"Okay, smartass, because obviously it's completely normal for an entire school to travel to the devil's balls for a field trip."

"Devil's balls?" Asher raised an eyebrow.

"Stop talking about my man parts!" Ryder huffed, and I couldn't help but chuckle. Dammit, Ryder was growing on me.

Conversation ended, though, when we reached the table in the corner. I gasped at the familiar face staring back at me.

"Ronan?"

"Princess?"

Asher rubbed his chin; Ryder looked annoyed.

"Do you two know each other?" he asked, eyes swinging from mine to Ronan's.

I answered, "No," just as Ronan answered with, "Yes."

"We met last night," Ronan supplied. "Though the little minx has yet to reveal her name to me."

"Phew," Ryder said, wiping invisible sweat from his forehead dramatically. "I thought it was just me."

"It *is* just you," I retorted.

He wiggled his eyebrows suggestively.

"Are you saying I'm the only guy you see?"

Rolling my eyes, I turned away from Ryder to face the rest of the table. Two unfamiliar guys stared back at me, one appearing transfixed and the other almost angry.

The first one had brown, almost red, curly hair just reaching his shoulders. His features were boyish, with emerald eyes framed by thick lashes and a tentative smile. As I considered him, his cheeks tinted red.

The second one had a fauxhawk, a few shades darker than Boy #1's. His eyes, unlike his friend's, were narrowed at me as if he could physically penetrate my skin. I didn't understand his animosity towards me, a virtual stranger, and it made me wonder if it was because I was intruding on bro-time. On their bro-meal or whatever it was called. Was there a code for it? Was a female not allowed to eat during this sacred time? Either way, I found myself glaring right back. For the briefest of moments, a smile graced Glarey's features before he immediately masked it. With what, you might ask. You guess it: a scowl. I'm pretty sure that was a standard emotion on Glarey's face.

"This is my friend Tamson," Asher introduced, gesturing towards the curly haired guy. "And this is Declan." This was directed towards Mr. Grumpy. Maybe the boy just needed food in his system.

Tamson offered a small smile, blushed, and then looked down at his menu. The back of his neck burned a bright red

So apparently Mr. Tam was a blusher. There was a lot that you could do with that type of information.

"So, princess, are you stalking me?" Ronan asked with a dramatic wink. I swear these boys never did anything half-assed. It was always with an elaborate flare, as if they were actors on stage.

"I prefer to say that I was following you without your

knowledge," I replied. Ronan threw back his head and roared with laughter.

"I like this girl. Can we keep her?"

"You like *every* girl," Asher muttered under his breath.

Ryder said, "I think Asher already called dibs. He spent the night with her." He sounded bitter at the prospect.

Declan's eyes whipped from where they were focused intently on Ryder's face to mine. If Ryder looked slightly annoyed, Declan looked positively furious.

Ronan sputtered, "What? Asher?" He pointed towards the boy in question. "Our sweet, innocent, virgin Asher?"

"Shut up!" Asher mumbled, whacking Ronan on the back of the head. "And no, we did not hookup."

At this, Ryder gasped in mock outrage.

"Did you lie to me, my little kitten?"

Raising my chin imperiously, I said, "First, don't call me that. And second, I decided I didn't like you, and so I wanted you to suffer."

Asher snorted, and Ronan laughed again.

"Why didn't you like me?" Ryder asked. He sounded oddly amused by my confession, as if he found me "cute" instead of serious. Men and their egos.

"You were cocky. Emphasis on the cock." I leaned forward to whisper conspiratorially. "It can't be that big to equivalate such an attitude. You must be compensating for *something*."

For a moment, the boys stared at me, too stunned to speak. As one, they howled with laughter garnering the attention of a few pedestrians eating nearby. Even grumpy ole Declan cracked a smile.

"I can assure you that my ego is justified," Ryder responded smoothly. "So, getting back to the matter at hand, if you're not dating Asher, does that mean you're single?"

Ronan thrust up a hand to interrupt.

"I would just like to point out that I saw her first."

Declan looked amused by this declaration while Asher just appeared annoyed.

"That's not the way it works," he huffed. "Besides, I technically saw her first."

I snorted. Guys were amusing…well, more amusing than girls who seemed to come pre-packaged with drama. To be honest, I never actually had a girl best friend – someone to do my hair and paint my toenails and whatever else girls do together. I'm 90% positive that it's not comparing dick sizes and harassing a poor female about her dating life. Hell, for all I knew, this was probably normal man-dude-bro-time conversation.

Smirking, I allowed my eyes to sweep over the men present. I would like to say that I was merely observing my prospective friends, but that would be a lie. I totally was checking them out. How could I not? They were all hot, even Tamson with his reddening cheeks and disheveled hair. Why did they have to be so attractive? They were really testing my self-control.

Shame.

"I don't date," I answered at last, disrupting their argument. Ryder blinked. He looked as if he wasn't sure if he believed my declaration. After a moment, an incredulous expression contorted his features.

"Like right now?"

"Like ever." I ran my hand over the glossy menu, an absent-minded gesture. "I don't want to be in a relationship."

Ryder seemed aghast – though I found that hilarious because he did not seem like the type of guy to do long-term relationships. More like one-night relationships, if you know what I mean. Men with their double standards and hypocritical judgements. As you could probably tell, I haven't had the best track-record with guys. I suppose that most of that could be contributed to D.O.D. and his string of business partners. They saw girls as easy, and we lived in an unfortunate society where the perpetrator was victimized, and the actual victim was blamed. It wasn't my fault that I couldn't trust men; it was my father's.

"Why not?" Ryder asked, diverting my attention.

I shrugged. There was really no way for me to confess the truth to a group of strangers. How does one say that she's afraid of getting close to people because they could get hurt? That she doesn't believing she's deserving of love?

Yeah, totally not first meeting conversation.

"You just haven't found the right guy," Ryder insisted, and my mind immediately flashed to Ducky. His eyes almost reminded me of Declan's, minus the whole stare-you-down-until-you-die sort of thing that Declan had going on. The two could've been related.

"Trust me. That's not the reason."

"Where's Calax?" Asher interrupted.

My body went cold at the strange name. How many people at this resort had that name? It was such a stupid name. An evil name...

"For the love of..." I muttered just as a strident voice demanded, "What the hell is she doing here?"

Plastering a pleasant (but fake) smile on my face, I turned towards the voice, already knowing that I would have to strain my head to make eye contact. Calax was a giant, a real monster of a man. His tousled brown hair grated his eyes which were – unsurprisingly – narrowed on me. He wore his customary scowl.

"Hello Callie. Looking lovely as ever this fine evening."

Calax pinched the bridge of his nose. This was his standard "trying to be patient with Adelaide" face. Well, excuse me. I *tried* to be nice.

"Addie, what are you doing here?"

There was an eruption of voices from the table.

"Your name is Addie?"

"*This* is Addie?"

"Well shit."

I didn't look to see whose words belonged to which voice. Calax's eyes remained locked on mine in an unspoken battle of dominance, and I would be damned if I let him win. Calax was, admittedly, a scary man. If I were to see him in a dark alleyway, I would probably piss my pants. With his shadowed face, black clothing, and towering frame, he could put even the strongest of people in cardiac arrest.

He was also my mortal enemy. Don't ask me why or how. He just was.

"*This* is Adelaide," Ryder sputtered. I didn't like the way he was saying my name – as if he was accusing me of something. Knowing Calax, that wouldn't be surprising. The entire table probably thought I was crazy. I mean, I probably *was*, but he didn't have to *tell* everyone.

"Judging by all the exclamations, I assume Callie told you so many wonderful things about me," I said, subtly giving Calax the middle-finger behind my back. The bastard snorted.

"Trust me. We hear a lot about you," Ryder said, smirking at Calax. I didn't even have to turn my head to know that the mountain man was glowering. Calax only had two expressions: a scowl and a semi-scowl. Semi, because I could've sworn that he would want to smile but was too stubborn to actually do it. Thus, a semi-scowl.

It occurred to me that, in just a matter of a few minutes, I had two people glaring daggers at me. That was a personal record. I really bring out the best in people.

"Calax is my nemesis," I announced after a moment. "Like the whole enemy, fall-and-crack-your-head-open sort of relationship going on."

Ryder and Ronan broke into laughter. It was Ronan who

spoke first, wiping tears out of his eyes. He turned towards Calax.

"You didn't mention that she hated you."

"He's a very hateable person," I pointed out. Calax grumbled inarticulately but slid into the booth beside me. His thigh touched mine, and I poked him in his muscled chest.

"Move over, Big Guy. I don't want to catch your cooties."

He ignored me, as always, and pressed his leg even closer to mine.

"Aw. No fair. How come Calax gets to sit so close to Princess?"

"Princess?" Calax grumbled, seeming annoyed by the nickname. Declan appeared upset that Calax was upset. So basically, everyone besides me was upset. A note to all my readers: if you want to make friends, make them cry first. Trust me.

Declan and Calax seemed to be engaged in some kind of macho stare-down. I would seriously never understand boys.

Smiling at Ronan, I said, "Calm yourself, Lucky Charms. I didn't ask for this big brute to sit by me."

"Did you just call me a big brute?" Calax asked, breaking eye contact with Declan.

"Did you just call me, Lucky Charms?" Ronan added. He ran his fingers through his tousled green hair.

"You have to admit that you look like a leprechaun."

"That is insultingly adorable." To the rest of the guys, Ronan pleaded, "Please? If you don't want to keep her, I will."

Calax shifted even closer to me at Ronan's words, and Declan's eyes zeroed in on the minuscule movement. Ugh. Boys.

"Nobody's keeping me," I interrupted. "Besides, I don't date."

The waitress picked that time to come up to our table.

She was an older woman who was, fortunately, immune to Ryder's charm (not that he didn't try).

"Doris, looking as beautiful as ever."

In answer, she merely wacked him with her notepad. It was official: Doris was the grandmother I never had.

The boys ordered quickly, but I took my time surveying the menu. So many choices...

"Okay, I'll have a cheeseburger with extra cheese. Like seriously, five slices would be perfect. And some onion rings...yes, onion rings sound amazing. Hmm...let me try a slice of your cherry pie. And a chocolate shake. Are your French fries good? It doesn't really matter. I'll try them anyway. Do you have cheese sauce for them? I'll take some of that. And coffee. Lots and lots of coffee." I closed my menu happily and handed it to the amused waitress. The boys all stared at me as if I had sprouted wings.

"What?" I asked. "Have you never seen a girl eat before?"

Ronan mock whispered to Asher, "And all I ordered was a salad to try to impress her."

Calax snorted. "Addie eats enough for an army."

"Are you calling me fat, Callie?" I asked, narrowing my eyes playfully. He scoffed.

"If anything, you need more meat on your bones."

"Don't go dissing my bones, Big Guy." In response, Calax stabbed my belly with his finger. I was almost positive that his finger rested on my stomach a second longer than necessary before he pulled it back and crossed his beefy arms.

"You're too skinny."

"Surprising," Ronan injected, "considering how much she eats."

"Hey!" I said, stomping my foot on the ground. "I'm feeling verbally attacked right now."

"Well maybe you should-" Whatever Calax was about to

say was cut off by a rumble. For a moment, I was frozen. What was that?

A violent tremor rocked my body forward. Glasses shattered, and somebody let out an ear-splitting squeal. I would like to say that that somebody was Calax, but that would be a lie. It may or may not have been me. The table trembled, collapsing in on itself like old, brittle paper.

Before I realized what was happening, not a hard feat, mind you, Calax had pushed me to the ground, his muscled body covering mine. An assortment of dishes and wall decorations rained down upon us. I was too stunned to move.

After what felt like hours, but was probably more like a couple of minutes, the shaking subsided.

"What the hell was that?" I heard Ronan ask, but my tongue felt like sandpaper in my mouth. I couldn't answer him, even if I wanted to.

We'd just survived an earthquake, that much was obvious. While earthquakes weren't unheard of in Michigan, they weren't necessarily common either. I could count on one hand the number of earthquakes I had experienced while living in this resort.

"Is everyone okay?" Asher questioned.

A chorus of affirmatives sounded around us.

It suddenly occurred to me that I was still sprawled on the ground, underneath the table, with Calax hovering over me. His weight rested on his forearms.

Squirming, I turned onto my back, so I could see his face. I couldn't understand why he had protected me. Was it a chivalrous gesture? Or was he trying to smother me with his body and make it look like an accident?

Despite my wishes, the expression on his face didn't appear murderous. It could almost be described as...tender. That was one word I never thought I'd use to describe that giant of a man. His lashes feathered against his cheekbones, and his breath left him in a smooth exhale. Before I realized what was happening, his calloused hand reached to brush my hair away from my face.

And there it was again. That *tenderness.*

"Are you okay?" he asked. That same hand curved around my jaw, thumb skimming across my cheek. His hand almost engulfed my entire face.

"I'm fine," I whispered.

This was a very strange moment for me. I didn't know how to behave, what to say. For as long as I could remember, Calax had hated me and I had hated him. We were Romeo and Juliet, but without the love or the whole dying thing. In a blink of an eye, we found ourselves balancing on a precariously strung tightrope. One wrong move, and we would both be thrown over the edge. I had to remember that Calax was my nemesis, even if his body elicited completely un-nemesis like feelings above me. Non-enemy feelings that were getting harder and harder...

Scrambling out from under him, I tripped over a toppled chair in my haste to get some space. As he climbed to his feet, his hardened...um...manhood drew my eyes before they flickered back to his face. My cheeks burned.

Earthquake. There was an earthquake. And the salt and pepper shakers broke. Oh dear god, not the salt and pepper shakers. How could we continue on?

That, ladies and gentlemen, was deflection at its finest.

"Are you okay, Princess?" Ronan asked, his fingers grazing my arm to turn me towards him. Ryder appeared over his shoulder, his brow furrowed in concern.

"Of course I'm okay," I scoffed. "What about you guys?"

"We're fine." That came, surprisingly, from Tamson. He brushed dust from his slacks and pushed his glasses further up his nose. I noticed, with some relief, that they weren't broken.

"Everybody stay calm!" An unfamiliar man called. I think he was the manager, though I couldn't recall his name. "Somebody should be here shortly."

I resisted the urge to roll my eyes.

Great. Just freaking great.

CHAPTER 4

*R*yder suggested we move our party to the lobby. I couldn't help but giggle at that. I had never been invited to a party (minus the elite affairs forced upon me by my precious parents), but I didn't think what we were doing constituted as a party. No, I am most certain, based on my extensive Netflix research, that parties do not involve sitting on couches and chairs while eyeing one another warily.

"Is everybody okay?" Asher asked for probably the one-hundredth time.

"Fine and dandy," responded Ryder, flashing me a cheeky grin. "All my organs are still in working order."

"Pervert," I muttered.

The only response came from the crackling flames from the fireplace. The heat it emitted was near stifling, but I was not brave enough to suggest moving the party elsewhere. See? Pun.

Spotting a familiar, gray-haired man hobbling through the expansive lobby, I jumped to my feet.

"Mr. Ackles! How is everyone? Are there any injuries?"

The resort's manager considered me with kind eyes. I

always thought Mr. Ackles was too good to work at such a place, too kind to be under the thumb of my malicious parents. He had a way about him, whether he was fussing at me for running down his halls or reminding me not to do drugs, that reminded me of a grandpa. If I had a grandpa, because I seriously believed my parents were hatched from the eggs of the devil, I would want him to be like Mr. Ackles.

"I just heard back from Gavin. There was one minor injury, but nothing else has been reported."

I let out a relieved breath at the information.

"And you? How are you?" I asked, surveying his tiny form. For as long as I could remember, Mr. Ackles walked with a limp. He told me once that he had gotten it from the war, and I knew that even the slightest bit of strain could cause him immense pain.

"I'm fine, darling." He waved his hand dismissively, though I didn't miss the slight wince as he attempted to amble back towards the elevator.

"You're not fine," I countered. "You need to rest. Go sit at the counter. Don't worry about anything besides getting yourself better."

"But your father-"

"I'll talk to my father. Go. Sit." Without breaking eye-contact, I pointed towards the mahogany counter situated at the far wall of the lobby. I knew that there was a stool directly behind it, though very few employees dared to sit on the job. Daddy was a mean son of a bitch, and his employees were well aware of his temper tantrums.

Mr. Ackles gave me an undecipherable look before nodding his head. Relief was evident in his eyes as he hobbled back towards the desk. I made sure to keep an eye on him until he was safely seated and engaged in conversation with one of the many guests demanding an explanation (though why people felt the need to reprimand the resort for a natural disaster was beyond my comprehension. Seriously, people were strange).

Turning back towards the boys, I saw them all staring at me with varying expressions of awe, though they quickly turned towards one another when they caught me looking. A tentative smile played on Calax's lips, but his eyes remained glued to Asher, acting as though he was paying attention to whatever the other was saying.

"Look," I began, sliding back into my seat between Ryder and Ronan (The R squared, as I liked to call them in my head). "Can we just admit that what happened in the diner was one big shit-fest? A shest?"

"A chest?" Tamson parroted, peeking at me through his mane of curly hair.

"A shest," I repeated. "S. H. E. S. T. It's my word for shit-fest."

"Do you do that a lot?" Ronan questioned. He brought his knuckles to his chin and sat his elbow on his knee as he surveyed me. "Make up words?"

"Yes," Calax, the bastard, responded for me. I threw a throw-pillow at him which he neatly dodged. Apparently undeterred by my anger, he continued, "Her mind is strange. I don't even understand what goes through her head half the time."

"First you call me fat, and now you call me dumb. Is this National Insult Adelaide Day? Because I'm pretty sure that day passed like two months ago. They had a whole parade and everything. I think my parents even got a piñata that looked exactly like me just so they could whack it with a stick without guilt. Unfortunately, no candy came out. Just guts. And blood. I think the piñata was alive."

There was a moment of stunned silence, and then Calax said, "See?"

The boys burst into laughter. If I wasn't a mature, young

lady, I would've given Calax the middle finger and then threatened to burn him alive at the stake. Instead, I walked over, hit his head, and then sat back down. *Maturely*.

"So, want to tell me why you guys are here?" I said, attempting to change the subject. Calax was rubbing at his head, eyes narrowed on me, and Ronan was on the floor in peals of laughter.

"Well, as we said before, we go to Highwood Prep. It's a private school a couple of miles from here," Ryder began.

"There was a fire in our dormitories," Asher continued, "so we used our admission fee to pay for a section of the resort as a replacement until the repairs are completed."

"Highwood Prep isn't just a high school," Ronan continued, finally collecting himself enough to move back towards his recliner. "It actually goes all the way to college. I think the youngest kids are about thirteen and the oldest are... what?...maybe twenty-one or so."

That explains all the boob jobs.

"What?" Tamson sputtered, face a deep, burgundy red.

"Just...the girls...at the pool...they definitely had boob jobs. I was wondering what type of parents would let high schoolers get such a big boob job – get it? Big? – anyway, it makes sense now that I know that some girls are over eighteen. They don't have to get their parents' permission. Not that I'm knocking a boob job or anything, I mean some people can totally rock them, but some just look really..." I trailed off, unable to coherently express my private thoughts. This was exactly why some things needed to remain silent. "How old are you guys?" I asked, desperate to change the subject. Again. I really needed to stop getting myself into such awkward situations.

"Well, Tamson over there is the baby. He's only seventeen. Asher and Ryder are both eighteen. Calax, as you know, is nineteen along with Declan and I," Ronan said, pointing at each face as he went along, as if I needed a reminder of their names.

It was one of the final names that I got stuck on. Declan.

Before I could stop myself, because, really, I had no filter, I asked, "Why doesn't he talk?"

There was a moment of silence, during which Declan met my eyes with a smoldering stare of his own. For once, he didn't seem upset with something I said, only startled. His hand moved in a flurry of motion. Sign language.

"Do you think she's playing ignorant or does she really not know?" he signed, though the question wasn't directed at me. Calax immediately responded.

"Trust me. I have known Addie for years. She can barely remember where a wall is at. She's oblivious, not cruel."

Rude.

"She's hot though," Ryder signed. *"I say that we keep her."*

"I already called dibs," Ronan broke in.

"I don't trust her," Declan said. *"She's shady."*

Asher added, *"Well, this conversation escalated quickly."*

"She's hot though."

"Kind of stupid."

"Not stupid. Just naive."

"A girl like her? Doubt it. And I doubt that she never had a boyfriend before. That was the worst way to put someone down I had ever heard."

Their words – excuse me, *motions* – blurred together so I had trouble keeping up with who signed what, too focused on their hands to notice. After a moment of letting them continue their "insult Addie" game, I broke in.

"You're right. Addie is *seriously hot. And stupid. And kind of crazy, to be honest. And no, she has never had a boyfriend. Good grief, you guys are pathetic."*

I finished my signing with a dramatic flip of my hair. The guys all gaped at me yet again. Even cold, unyielding, asshole

Declan appeared sheepish and flustered. Good. Served him right for talking about me – damn it, *signing* about me.

"Now if you guys are done being dick faces, I am going to go. You know, do some shady shit and all that. I call it shat. Shady Shit. And yes, that is an Adelaide original word. And no, you cannot use it."

Aware that their eyes remained on me, staring at me like fish out of water, I gave them the universal F-you sign. It made me feel better.

CHAPTER 5

*T*was exactly thirteen minutes and twenty-six seconds late to the meeting.

I know. I'm a smartass. Sue me.

From the glower D.O.D. gave me, one would think that I was two days late and had arrived wearing a fedora dipped in the blood of my enemies. Okay, maybe Daddy would've appreciated the whole blood thing. He had always been a sick, twisted bastard.

He held his hands in front of him, folded on top of his desk. To anyone that didn't know him, the gesture might've been considered relaxed. Comfortable.

But I could see the vein bulging in his forehead and the noticeable grinding of his teeth.

"I'm sorry," I began immediately once I entered his stuffy office. I learned at a young age that an apology was always the best first step when it came to my father. Correction, it was the *only* step. "With the earthquake and everything-"

"I don't want to hear your excuses," he snapped. "Sit."

He pointed to a plush, leather chair directly in front of his mahogany desk. As I made my way there, I noticed the occupant of the second seat. I recognized the receding hairline and beady black eyes instantly.

Buttlicker. He had returned to lick more butts...my father's, I imagined, because D.O.D. wouldn't allow him to kiss it.

Daddy stared at me, eyes penetrating, for a few seconds longer before turning towards Buttlicker. He then began discussing their contract, and I deflated in relief. Maybe, just maybe, he'd forgiven me for my transgression. After all, it wasn't as if I could control the weather. Not even my dad could, though I supposed that he wished it.

I realized the mistake of my earlier relief when the meeting concluded. I had spent the hour nodding occasionally; the majority of what they discussed went through one ear and out the other. Oh well.

I had just climbed to my feet, stretching my taut muscles, when I noticed two sets of eyes trained on me. One was darkened in anger, another with lust. I'm sure you could guess which eyes belonged to which psycho.

"You know that I hate intolerance, Adelaide," D.O.D.. reprimanded, his tone cold and calm. I hated when he used this voice - it was like the tranquility before a storm. Frankly, it was his shit-your-pants type of voice that instilled justifiable fear in anyone who heard it.

"I was on my way to the meeting," I lied (because who would want to show up an hour early?). "I told you. It was the earthquake-"

The, not altogether unexpected, slap interrupted my excuse. I barely even winced when my head snaked sideways. No, I wouldn't give him the satisfaction of seeing me in pain. It was something that I could call my own. My pain. When did I start coveting pain? God, maybe I was sick.

"Don't lie to me." Spit flew from my dad's mouth. Buttlicker, still leaning back in the seat next to me, smiled smugly. "I have a source that said they saw you whoring yourself out."

For a moment, all I could do was blink in disbelief. "Whoring myself...?"

Slap.

I rubbed at my cheek. From the self-satisfied grin on Buttlicker's face, I could hazard a guess at the identity of that source.

You stupid perverted son of a bitch-

Buttlicker's face reddened, and I realized I had spoken aloud. Buttlicker confirmed this when he leaned forward to slap my other cheek. Yay! At least I'd have matching bruises. It's all about symmetry, my friends.

It took considerable restraint to stop myself from cutting off Buttlicker's balls and feeding them to D.O.D.. Heaven knows that D.O.D. preferred the pickle over the muffin, if you know what I'm saying.

"Take off your clothes," D.O.D. sneered. Knowing I was already in trouble, I figured it wouldn't hurt to poke the bear a little more. I had so many suppressed emotions, so much pent-up anger, whirling inside me that demanded release.

"Wow. I knew you were a psycho, but I never imagined incest on your list of perversions. Is that how you came into being? Were your parents brother and sister?"

The following punch was hard, landing right in the stomach. I doubled over.

Yes. *More*.

I enjoyed the pain. It reminded me of what I often forgot - that I was alive. Sort of alive, at least. I mean, I knew that my heart beat and I continued to breathe, I wasn't living. I couldn't even remember what that felt like. The closest I had come to happiness was earlier today with the guys, the few times I had talked with Calax, and my friendship with Ducky. All I had now was the pain, and though not ideal, I would take it over the nothingness I often wanted to succumb to.

I barely paid Buttlicker any mind as he ripped my dress off. His hands groped me, fondling my breasts like the pervert he was. Fortunately, he left my bra and underwear on.

From this angle, I knew my dad could see the scars marring the length of my arm. It was impossible not to. They etched themselves into my skin like an ugly tattoo. A few, the ones closest to my wrist, began to well up, blood rising to the surface, for the cuts had yet to heal.

My dirty little secret.

Without speaking, Dad grabbed my wrist and dragged me out of the office. We received a few stares from employees as I was dragged down the hall, through the break room, and into the back door of the restaurant.

The kitchen was bustling with activity. Chefs slaved over stoves and pans in an attempt to cater to the dinner crowd. A few waitresses and waiters lurked around, shouting directions at the cooks and grabbing plates. Even an earthquake couldn't stop the resort from running.

I spotted a familiar mound of tousled blond hair.

Please no. Not him.

I turned my head away, telling myself that if I couldn't see him, he couldn't see me. I channeled the stories I read when I was younger. The ones where the kid hid herself under her blankets to ward off the monsters (as if a fluffy blanket could repel a monster. Seriously. Sleep with a knife like a normal person).

The kitchen quieted down, the chatter and strident voices diminishing almost immediately.

Keep talking. Nothing to see here. Just a poor, bruised girl about to receive her punishment. Completely normal.

I honestly couldn't tell you if I had spoken that thought

aloud. I'm sure the pitying expressions would've stayed the same no matter what I said.

D.O.D. walked briskly over to an iron-top stove and flicked the dials to the highest settings. Buttlicker squeezed my arm, propelling me towards my father, while his free hand groped my bottom.

"What the hell, you pervert!" Asher yelled, trying to make his way to me, but he was intercepted by two cooks. Asher was young and angry, but he was no match for the two chefs that looked as if they ate more food than they made.

They knew what was going to happen. Hell, Chef Larry and I were old friends.

My dad merely stared at me without saying a word. I knew what he wanted.

Bracing my body, D.O.D. placed my arms on the stove. The pain was immediate. Blistering. My skin felt as if it was splintering from my body, shattering like cracked glass. I screamed in agony, instinct driving me to fight to remove myself from the source of the pain. D.O.D. held my body tightly, refusing to allow me to nudge an inch. I was trapped.

"Let her go! Stop! Stop it!" Asher screamed, thrusting against the men that held him. More employees had joined the fray.

Through my haze of pain, I felt something that resembled relief. Never, in all my years of existence, had anyone ever fought for me before. I always faced every trial alone. Turning my head, I met Asher's tear-filled eyes and gave him a shaky smile. This stranger, this shy, sweet boy, was in my corner when everybody else had abandoned me.

His was the last face I saw before the world faded into darkness.

≈

I woke up to someone sobbing.

For a moment, I thought that the sound was coming from me. I didn't think I was crying, but who the hell knew anymore. Mixed with the whole sobbing symphony, I heard a steady beeping. Confused, I twisted in the bed, and the beeping noise began to sound at intermittent intervals.

Huh. A heart-monitor.

The sound immediately began to slow itself once I came to that conclusion. Voices, though stunted by what was probably a door, floated to me.

"What the fuck are we going to do?" The voice sounded familiar, and it took me a second to place where I had heard it before. Ronan, the unicorn tattooed, green-haired, leprechaun.

What was he doing here?

"I didn't know it was this bad," a choked voice added. I didn't even need to think to know who this voice belonged to. Calax. He sounded ragged, as if...as if he had been the one I heard crying.

I snorted at the ridiculousness of that thought. If he was crying, then it was probably because I survived. The bastard seemed to hate me more than my own parents did.

"You didn't see it," Asher said. I had to strain to hear his quiet voice. "The entire staff knew what was going to happen. They fucking knew, and they did nothing to stop it. They told me that shit like this happens all the time. Not a week goes by when she isn't covered in bruises or casts. Hell, they even told me her parents often send sleazy fuckers to her room at night..." His voice broke off in anguish, and my heart fluttered at his obvious distress at my situation. Sure, I knew that my parents' treatment of me wasn't normal, but to hear someone else vocalize it, to condemn the people who repeatedly put me through hell, almost made me smile, like the twisted fucker they'd created. I never had anyone care about me or advocate on my behalf before. The feeling was strange but not entirely unpleasant.

An explosion of noise met Asher's confession. Something shattered, and I could only hope it was something expensive. Maybe a nice old vase.

"You were with her for years!" Ryder exploded at someone - I'm assuming Calax because he's the only one I knew before yesterday. "How could you not have known?"

Ryder was rewarded with a strangled sound.

"Enough!" This forceful voice surprised me the most, mainly because I didn't recognize it. "I know tensions are running high, but we need to keep our crap together. Now how is it going with the police?"

My mouth - well, my mental mouth because I totally wasn't going to move - dropped open when I finally placed that voice. The last few times I'd heard it, it had been nothing more than a timid murmur, but that husky timbre was unmistakable. *Tamson.*

Who would've thought that shy boy had a bossy streak?

Maybe he just behaved like that around me. After all, I was a girl. Or maybe, just maybe, I had gotten him completely wrong. For all I knew, he kept a house full of playgirls bending over to please him. Literally. Because, you know, in this fantasy Tamson was a kinky son of a -

Focus, Adelaide! I mentally scolded myself.

I concentrated once more on their conversation.

"...under their thumb," Ryder was saying, irritated. "The fuckers laughed when I called."

Laughed? Who did they call? Hopefully it wasn't the police because they were-

"Crooked cops," Ronan sneered.

Yup. What he said.

I made the idiotic mistake of calling them once, after a particularly bad beating. My arm had been broken in more than two spots, and I had a punctured lung. The doctor of the resort, an aging, malicious man who was blinded by this loyalty to my parents, had announced that I was lucky to be alive.

As if it were *my* fault my dad decided to beat me.

So I had called the cops. I was many things, but I wasn't stupid enough to take chances with my life. The conversation started off simple enough until I had given my name and address. All at once, the operator declared there was nothing she could do to help me and hung up.

Not even an hour later, D.O.D. punished me for attempting to get in contact with the authorities.

"I agree with Declan," Asher said. "I don't give a damn about our supervisors. We need to change the mission. All in favor?"

A chorus of "ayes" rang out.

What mission? And what supervisor?

I wanted to yell at them for not providing more information. What's the point of eavesdropping if you don't understand half the conversation?

But as my mind spun, drowsiness threatened to pull me under. The darkness was alluring and seemed to be calling for me.

I answered the call and allowed it to consume me.

THE NEXT TIME I woke up, I was actually able to open up my eyes.

The first thing I noticed was that I was in a hospital - the resort's hospital, no surprise there. The familiar white walls and pungent aroma of bleach made the room unwelcoming. How many times had I been here? It struck me deep when I couldn't recall the exact number.

The heart monitor still beat its annoying tune, and someone still sobbed nearby.

What the actual -?

I twisted my head, a surprisingly painful movement, to see Calax in the chair beside my bed. His large frame looked awkward in such a cramped, tiny space, and I wondered if he had gotten stuck.

He held his head in his hands, and his body shook as sobs racked his body forward. It didn't make any sense. Giants didn't cry. He should've been smiling or licking blood off his fingers or lapping up intestines...

Calax's eyes flickered towards me.

Whoops. Must've spoken that aloud.

"You're awake," he said breathlessly. "How do you feel?"

"Like my dad beat the shit out of me, and then burnt me over a stove like a pot of spaghetti," I teased with a light smile. Calax did not seem to find it funny; his scowl deepened.

"This isn't fucking funny!" As if his agitation demanded a physical response, he jumped from his seat.

"It's fine, Calax," I whispered. "This happens all the time. I'll feel better in a few days, tops. I'm used to it."

I had meant to comfort him - though I didn't know why because he hated me, and likewise, I hated him - but my words only appeared to make him angrier. A hundred different emotions flickered across his handsome face before settling on despair.

"You shouldn't have to get used to something like this." All at once, as if his legs couldn't hold his body up, he collapsed onto his knees before me. "Baby, I am so sorry this happened to you. It shouldn't...you shouldn't have..." Unshed tears glistened in his wide eyes. Somehow, that vulnerability made him seem less like an evil giant, and more like a handsome young man. I had the irresistible urge to wrap my arms around his thick neck and cuddle against him.

Woah. Where did that come from?

I settled for awkwardly patting him on the head like a dog.

"Calax," I began softly. When my voice faltered over that one word, I cleared my throat and tried again. "Calax, you have to understand that there's nothing you or I can do about this. My parents are...well, they're powerful people. And obviously they're not the good guys. I know-"

"You don't know shit if you think I'm just going to sit back and allow you to be tortured!" Calax snapped, rage-filled eyes meeting mine. I knew his anger wasn't directed at me, but I didn't like seeing him upset. Absently, I used two fingers to smooth over the furrow between his eyebrows. I moved those same two fingers to his lips, turning them up. He shivered beneath my touch, and I wondered if my hands were cold.

Of course, that meant I had to keep them on his face longer. For torturous reasons only. Nothing else.

Calax sighed deeply and turned his face into my palm. Was that-

Were his lips pressing against the skin there?

"I promise that we'll figure something out, Baby. You don't have to go through this alone anymore."

Somehow, despite everything, I believed him.

"I know, Big Guy. I know."

THE THIRD TIME I woke up - because third time's a charm - I realized males surrounded me. Hot males.

It's official. I must've died and gone to Heaven.

Deep chuckles greeted that statement.

Chicken shit. Butt groper, piece of-

"Princess, you're doing it again," Ronan said, still chuckling.

I huffed. "Oh please. You guys find it adorable."

"She's not wrong," Ryder pointed out and was simultaneously whacked in the head by the two grumps of the group, Calax and Declan.

"Ow!" he whined. "Addie! They hit me!"

His lower lip protruded out into a pout, and I nearly fell off the bed in my hysterical fit.

"You...look like...a constipated puppy!" I managed to wheeze out, very eloquently mind you. The rest of the boys burst into laughter at my statement, even Declan. Ryder's face flamed.

"That face usually works on the females," he whispered to Asher, but that only made me laugh harder. Those females must've been blind or desperate. I said as much to Ryder.

The boys doubled over in laughter, and Ryder leaned forward to pinch my arm.

"You're such a little shit!"

"Hey!" Calax bellowed, grabbing Ryder by the back of his shirt. "Careful of her injuries!"

I rolled my eyes. "It's fine, Callie. It's not like a little pinch is going to cause internal bleeding."

He merely glared at me in response.

"So," I began, attempting to pull myself up into a sitting position. I probably looked like a dying fish on land for all the good that did me. Ronan, chuckling under his breath, finally helped me up and placed a pillow behind me. At least someone knew how to behave like a gentleman, minus the whole laughing thing.

Before I could continue my thought, though I honestly didn't know where I was going with it in the first place,

Tamson piped up from the back. He had, once again, reverted back to the shy, sweet boy I had initially met.

"How are you feeling? Do you need me to get the doctor?" At his words, the mood instantly sobered.

"I can grab you a water," Asher added. "Or would you like something to eat?"

Smiling cheekily, I said, "It's official. Tam and Asher are my two favorites. I mean, come on. Asher offered me food not once, but twice. How could he not get top honors? And Tam's just a sweetie."

Both of their faces turned bright red which only reaffirmed the whole favoritism thing. I loved it when they blushed.

Ryder growled at my words.

"Oh, it's on, Kitten."

"Challenge accepted," Ronan added, cracking his knuckles.

"Whatever, drama queens...or in this case, leprechauns. Now back to my question...which I may have forgotten. Okay, so I never actually asked it to begin with, but it was important. Just give me a moment. One second."

"Is she always like this?" Ronan mocked-whispered to Calax.

Calax grunted an affirmative.

Snapping my fingers together, I was pleased with myself when I finally remembered what I was going to say. It was so obvious that I felt kind of stupid for needing to think about it. More stupid than usual, anyway.

"Why are you guys here?"

The boys blinked at me.

"That was the question you struggled so hard to remember?" Ryder asked in disbelief. I gave him the finger.

"This is why you're not my favorite."

"Nooo!" he whined. "I take it back, you intelligent goddess."

"Flattery will get you nowhere."

"It seems like she's immune to your charm," Asher muttered with a smirk. I, once again, nearly fell off the bed in laughter.

"Ryder doesn't have charm!" I gasped, giggling. Ryder surged forward, probably to pinch me again, but Calax restrained him.

"Boys," I cooed, flashing a shit-eating grin in their direction. "Why don't you kiss and makeup already?"

Calax and Ryder froze, exchanged horrified looks, and jumped apart as if their lives depended on it.

"Ignoring those shit for brains, why wouldn't we just want to spend time with you?" Asher asked. I stared at him incredulously.

"Uh...because you don't know me, and I'm certifiably insane."

The boys gave me a look for that one. Huffing, I said, "Is this about the whole incident? Are you guys playing body-guard now or something?"

If I expected guilt to appear in their expressions, I was sorely mistaken. They faced me with what I could only describe as resolve.

Well, fuck.

"Incident?" Ronan snorted. "You can't really say that what happened was only an incident. What those sick bastards did to you...."

"You can't get involved!" I hissed, not even caring when my voice came out in a desperate plea. "You don't understand what my family will do to you-"

"And you don't seem to understand what they do to you," Calax broke in. Before I could retort, he grabbed my hand. I expected his hand to feel rough on my skin, but despite his many callouses, his touch was unexpectedly gentle. "Or maybe you do understand," he murmured. His finger traced one of the many scars adorning my arm.

"Did you do this to yourself?" Asher asked, his voice sounding uncharacteristically loud in the sudden quiet of the room. Everybody seemed to await my answer with bated breaths.

My voice was just as low when I responded with, "It's none of your business."

This felt too intimate, too private, to share with a group of strangers. It was my pain, *mine*, and it was a secret I'd managed to keep for years. Didn't I deserve to have something all to myself? Something that was mine and mine alone? I was both terrified and angry that these boys had taken that from me.

From their anguished expressions, they were able to pick apart my words and uncover the truth.

Refusing to wallow in the pity party about to happen, I clapped my hands.

"Now back to the important issues. You guys. And what I mean by that is you guys getting the hell out of here as fast as you can. No arguments? Good. Now leave. Pack your bags. I'm sure you can find a nice little hotel to house your sorry asses until your school is fixed."

The boys surprised me by chuckling. They actually chuckled, as if they found me amusing when I had been deadly serious.

"Not happening, Princess."

"We're staying with you, Kitten."

"You're so adorable when you think we're going to leave."

I huffed, crossing my arms over my chest. There was a slight sting from the burns, now wrapped in bandages, but nothing I couldn't live with. The drugs helped to numb the pain. Speaking of drugs...

Maybe I could get my hands on a drug I could use to knock them out. Granted, it would be difficult to carry their fat asses (muscular, well-defined asses) out of the resort, but I had connections. I mean, it wouldn't count as kidnapping if I was doing it for their own good, right?

A hand waving in front of my face interrupted my musings..

Jolting back, I turned towards Declan.

His hands moved rapidly as he signed to me.

"You're an idiot if you think we'll leave you after everything that happened. Now quit your bitching and allow us to help you."

All I could do was stare at him, stunned. Slightly breathless, I said, "That was the longest sentence you have ever signed to me in my life. Does this mean we're best friends now?"

He rolled his eyes at me. Of course that meant we were best friends. Only best friends would roll their eyes at one another.

Totally nailed it.

"Do you ever take things seriously?" Tamson asked with sincerity. It threw me for a loop, and I paused to consider my response before speaking.

"Sometimes, but it hurts me more when I do," I admitted. When the guys gave me flabbergasted expressions, I hurried to explain. "I have spent my entire life failing to meet my parents' expectations. As you can see, I'm punished almost daily for these failures. Some days are worse than others. Because of this, I've never had any friends or anyone to confide in. Well, the one friend I did have was killed in a car accident." Tears burned my eyes at the memory, and I heard a sharp intake of breath. I didn't look to see which boy made the sound. "It was my fault. Everything is always my fault, because I bring it on myself - that's what my parents drilled into me. If I so much as sat the wrong way, I would get beaten. If I talked to one of the residents, my father would send one of his business partners to my room..." I trailed off as I noticed how hard Calax gripped the hospital chair. His eyes were unfocused, his breathing ragged. None of the guys looked any better after my confession. Each wore varying degrees of anger, horror, disgust, and sadness. I was almost grateful when I didn't spot pity in their kaleidoscope of emotions.

I wouldn't be able to handle that.

Swallowing, I hurried to continue before I lost my nerve. "I think I just gave up. If I choose to take everything seriously, to drown in my sorrow, I may never get back up again. God, it feels like I'm dying almost every day. I can't breathe at points. But I accepted my life, and I accepted the mask that I must wear to survive it. Instead of breaking, I make it into a joke. It may be a twisted way of handling things, but it keeps me sane, or somewhat close to it. I wouldn't be able to smile without it."

I let out ragged a breath. I hadn't meant to share as much as I did. I couldn't even tell you why I had. The words just spewed from my mouth like a verbal freight train. Maybe it was some innate need inside of me, a need that I didn't fully understand, that craved human companionship.

Acceptance.

Maybe I had spoken because these were feelings I had never dared put into words before because I had nobody to listen.

Or maybe, just maybe, it was because the last remaining grip I'd had on my sanity disappeared the moment my arms hit the stovetop.

"Addie," Ryder said. Tears welled in his eyes as he stared at me. "Nobody, and I mean nobody, should go through everything you did. You are so incredibly strong." His strong hand cupped mine, swallowing it whole.

"You don't have to worry about being alone anymore. We're your friends now, and we always look after our own," Asher added. I pushed back the tears that threatened to spill.

"You don't even know me," I pointed out huskily. I was an ugly crier, with snot and slobber and everything. They didn't want to see that. I didn't know how some girls could cry and still manage to look like freaking goddesses.

I bet Elena had a pretty cry, that bitch.

"I know you took the fall for me the other day at the restaurant, despite knowing that you would be punished," Asher whispered.

"I know that you're a stubborn brat that I want to learn more about," added Ryder.

Declan waved his hand once again to get everyone's attention.

"You can't blame yourself for everything. I know you believe that your friend-" Whatever he was about to say was cut off by a scream.

CHAPTER 6

*T*he boys all jumped to their feet and immediately surrounded my bed. The movement was so smooth, so rehearsed, that I had to wonder if they had done it before. Or perhaps they were just telepathic and could communicate in one another's minds.

Calax and Ronan broke away from the group to press their bodies against the door, one on either side.

If they thought I was some damsel in distress in need of saving, they were mistaken.

Pulling the IV out of my arm and disconnecting the heart monitor, I ambled to my feet. The pain in my arms wasn't as bad now, a dull ache that thrummed throughout my body. Ignoring the guy's protests, I grabbed a scalpel off the table and steadied it in front of me. It wasn't the greatest weapon, but it was sharp.

I liked sharp things.

"Dammit, Addie!" Calax mouthed at me, but he didn't charge over and try to stop me. Progress.

My smug smile faded as another ear-splitting scream

echoed through the hospital. My muscles locked together at the horrendous sound.

Calax and Ronan exchanged a look that made words unnecessary. As one, Ronan moved to open the door, and Calax released a gun from his holster.

A gun? What in the actual-

Calax stood in the doorway, aiming the gun to the left and then to the right - you know, that thing cops do in movies before they announce that a room is clear - and did a weird gesture with his hand.

Apparently, that wasn't the come-out-and-follow-me signal, though you could've fooled me. So, of course, I was the idiot that stepped out of the room and into the dimly lit hallway.

In my defense, I totally thought he was telling us to follow him.

The first thing I saw was the blood. Illogical as it sounds, I couldn't help but think that somebody had spilt cranberry juice on the hospital floor. There was no conceivable way that the mess before me could be blood. Did a human even have that much blood in their body?

Seemingly, the answer to that question is yes, yes indeed, for only a few feet away laid the mangled corpse of the resort's doctor. His stomach had been torn out, guts and other unsavory substances spilling out of him like cotton from a stuffed-animal. That wasn't the strangest thing though.

That was horrifying, yes, and slightly bizarre, but it wasn't what caused me to tremble in fear. I had seen death before, and though gruesome, his body was nothing new.

No, what terrified me was the second figure leaning over Dr. What's-His-Name. From this angle - and it had to be the angle because the alternative was too disgusting to comprehend - it looked as if Buttlicker was eating him.

Three things happened in a very quick succession.

First, I must've made a noise, whether it was a gasp, an intake of breath, or a whimper, I couldn't entirely determine, but Buttlicker's head whipped in my direction.

It was him...but it wasn't him. His eyes were the color of garnet stones, an unnatural red that contrasted with the white surrounding his eyes. His face looked cracked, as if it was precious glass that had been dropped one too many times. The jagged lines curved steeply down each cheek in an asymmetrical design. The skin around his neck was red and bloody.

Before I could even think to scream, he charged.

I would like to say that what happened next I'd done on purpose. I would like to say that I had been totally kickass and managed to defeat him with my ninja moves.

No, what happened was a complete and utter accident. The boys yelled out, with Ronan warning Calax to not shoot me by mistake, when Buttlicker pounced.

In my panic, I lifted my hands in a defensive maneuver, forgetting that I still held the scalpel. He fell over top of me, and the scalpel lodged itself in his throat.

I think I'm the only human alive that can accidentally stab someone.

A disgusting black tar exploded from the exposed wound. Buttlicker let out a series of inarticulate cries, hands reaching desperately for me.

The boys pulled him off me, but I barely processed that snippet of information.

I had killed someone. I had killed someone I knew. I didn't know how to deal with that knowledge. Instead of anger or guilt, I felt almost empty. I didn't like the feeling, the nothingness that promised pain. The urge to hurt myself hit me in a near palpable wave.

And what was that black substance oozing from his neck?

And why was he still moving, still wiggling, even after I had stabbed him? His eyes looked feral, enraged.

I had never seen anything like him before.

"Are you okay? Princess, breathe for me. You need to breathe. Take deep breaths."

I complied with his instructions almost mechanically.

"Good job. Good job, Princess. You're doing just fine."

Through my erratic spurts of breath, I caught sight of Ronan's terrified eyes. Was he terrified of me? Because I killed someone?

The thought only made me freak out more.

"Guys, what the hell is going on over there?" Ronan asked, not taking his eyes off me. His hand rubbed soothing circles into my back as he occasionally reminded me to breathe.

Easier said than done.

"I don't know what the fuck this thing is." Ryder's strained voice came from somewhere in front of me, hidden behind Ronan's bulky frame. "This is Walking Dead level shit right here."

"We need to call this in," Tamson added, sounding shaken.

"I killed someone." The words left my mouth in a broken whisper. "I'm a murderer. Oh god. I'm going to vomit."

Before I even finished my sentence, said vomit exploded like a volcano eruption. Ronan, for his part, didn't look away or even crinkle his nose in disgust. He continued to pat my back soothingly with one hand while the other hand pulled my hair out of my face. I was mortified to realize that my vomit had hit the unexpected bullseye...of his shoes.

"You didn't kill anyone," Ronan said softly. "It was self-defense, and he was still alive before Calax shot him dead."

Shot? Calax?

I hadn't even heard a gun go off.

"I don't think..." I gasped out, but then clamped my mouth shut when I realized I didn't know how to put my thoughts into words. I tried again. "I think he was sick or something. Did you see his face? His eyes? Oh god, what happened to him?"

Roman's hand tightened marginally in my hair, the grip more pleasurable than painful. He released it with a heaving breath.

"I don't know. I don't know."

$\mathcal{T}$he next few hours were a blur. One minute turned into the next which turned into the next. I remained motionless as my father's security arrived at the medical center, guns drawn.

The boys moved into a protective circle around me. I was too weak, too numb, to tell them that they didn't need to baby me.

But, maybe I did. After all, I could barely stand on my own two feet without collapsing. The only thing that kept me upright was Ronan's hand around my waist. It was both a mental comfort and a physical one. I was sure I would've fallen face first if he hadn't been there to hold me up.

My heart beat erratically as the body was removed and questions were asked. I don't remember what I said. Probably something stupid like "Buttlicker".

The doctors arrived shortly after the security. I didn't recognize them, but from the way they surrounded my father, I reasoned they must've worked for him. I was put into a room separate from the males, and the lady doctor asked me to strip off my clothes.

I felt immensely relieved that it wasn't some pervy old male attempting to cop a feel. That had happened to me once. Apparently, Dr. Johnson wasn't a real doctor.

After I washed off the blood, the lady doctor, who didn't provide her name, searched me for any injuries. She poked and prodded me to the point that I wondered if I had been abducted by aliens. She rebandaged my arms, her brow furrowing with something akin to disapproval, but did not comment on the red, raised skin.

When she finally dismissed me, I saw Ryder sitting in the waiting room, playing on his phone.

"How are you doing?" he asked when he saw me emerge. I was still dressed only in a hospital gown, the flimsy material doing very little to cover my body, yet I didn't feel sexualized in any way (surprising, consider that this was Ryder). A look of tender anxiety softened his handsome face.

"Usually I like stuff in my butt," I deadpanned. When Ryder began choking on his own spit, I added, "Too much?"

Despite my light words, I couldn't erase the image of Buttlicker in my mind. For some reason, it occurred to me that I didn't know his real name. I didn't know if it made me a horrible person or a sane one when I realized that I didn't want to know.

In my mind, I saw his eyes, the whites surrounding a red abyss. The feral snarl marring his features. The black, almost inky, blood pooling around him.

Had he felt any pain when he died? I imagined that his death hadn't been pleasant. He had been stabbed and, evidently, shot. How long had he been alive before death finally claimed him?

Ronan assured me it wasn't my fault, but that didn't stop the guilt. It felt pronounced and all-consuming, as if something heavy was pressing on my chest.

Suffocating me.

Was this what it felt like to be buried alive? Was there any relief?

One part of my mind scoffed at that word. Relief. No matter what Ronan said, I stabbed a man and, unintentionally or not, killed him. A life had been cut short because of me. Did I deserve relief? No.

I caused Ducky's death and now Buttlicker's. I deserved whatever punishment the universe wished to inflict upon me.

I got separated from the guys once again sometime during the interrogation. That was okay. I didn't deserve their friendship or their comfort.

No outside help came during the investigation. There were no police, no doctors besides my dad's hired staff, no FBI.

The conclusion they came to was simple: ecstasy. He had been on drugs, they told me, and wasn't in his right mind. I had questioned whether ecstasy could cause black marks on faces, cracks throughout skin, or blood red eyes. They had just exchanged wary glances before assuring me again that everything had been handled.

Hours later, I found myself sprawled across my bed. My eyes were heavy, but I found that only nightmares greeted me when I slept. It was beginning to get difficult to discern between reality and fantasy; both were hell.

I barely flinched when I heard footsteps pounding through my kitchen, heading towards my bedroom. When my door slammed against the wall, I didn't even blink.

You deserve this, a sly voice whispered inside my head. *Murderer*.

Ducky's face flashed through my head, and I stifled a sob. I was beginning to see his face everywhere again.

"What the hell did you think you were doing?" Dad demanded. Before I could even speak, he grabbed my foot and pulled me from the bed. My body clunked against the rail, head turning at an unnatural angle. Pain. I felt the pain. It broke through the hazy sheen like tiny, penetrating needles. More. I needed more.

"Stupid!" Punch. "Bitch!"

His hand fisted in my hair, pulling it back. The pressure made me whimper, but I quickly tried to keep it contained. My body ached everywhere - my back hurt from yesterday, my cheekbones stung, my scalp felt as if it were on fire (ironic, considering it was my back that had gotten burnt).

"He attacked me," I managed to wheeze out between kicks to my stomach. From the darkening of his eyes, I realized that was the incorrect thing to say. In his eyes, the man couldn't do anything wrong. It was my fault.

Always my fault.

After one more kick to my midsection, he sauntered away as if he had no care in the world. As if he did not just beat the crap out of his only daughter.

The tears flowed down my cheeks now that I was alone and could be vulnerable. Would I cry in front of my dad? Hell no. Would I cry now that he was gone?

Well if my snot was any indication, then yes. I couldn't always act strong, and I didn't want to. Just once, I wanted to fall and not worry that I would get stabbed by swords on the way down. An impossible feat, I was beginning to realize.

After drowning some aspirin to placate the pain, and I changed into a pair of sweatpants and a sweatshirt. The clothing did nothing to obscure the bruises darkening my cheeks and neck, but it provided me with some semblance of a shelter.

Still, I couldn't hide my limp as I wandered down the hall.

I didn't know where I was going nor, did I care. Half of me wanted to go to my secret pool, but I didn't want to run into any more annoying boob ladies with their shrill voices and their...well...fake boobs that made me self-conscious. Damn tears trailed unchecked down my cheeks as I walked from hallway to hallway.

A few guests met my gaze before quickly turning away, and the employees couldn't even meet my eyes. It was always the same story with abuse: everyone was too much of a coward to do anything, myself included. It wasn't as if I was unused to surviving alone, but it still caused an uncomfortable lump to well up in my throat. For once, I wanted someone to stand up for me as Asher had done before.

Preoccupied with my admittedly depressing thoughts, I didn't see the person in front of me until I plowed into him.

Looking back, I wondered if it was chance or fate. Why else would we be happening to walk down the same hallway, at the same time of night?

Sniffing, I turned my face up blindly to meet Declan's dark eyes.

His mouth opened - probably to call me out for not paying attention where I was walking - but his expression shattered upon seeing me. He took a horrified step backwards as if my appearance was a physical repellence.

I wanted to growl. I didn't need, nor did I want, his damn pity.

Dozens of emotions flitted across his normally impassive eyes until they settled on determination, if determination even was an emotion. If anything, his eyes looked as if they were made of steel, and his expression was almost angry. Not at me, but at the world.

Briskly, he made one motion with his hand.

Come.

I didn't know if I was more surprised at him for talking to me or me for following him.

We didn't speak as we walked down hallway after hallway, stopping occasionally to allow a guest to pass us. I appreciated it; I didn't want any more people to see me than necessary.

When we finally reached our destination, I grabbed his arm to get his attention.

"The game room?" I questioned, glancing at the surprisingly empty room. "What are we doing here?"

He ignored me and proceeded towards an air hockey table in the center of the modest room.

Like the wannabe beach, this room had long since been abandoned in place of a high-tech, shiny arcade located a few halls down. I much preferred this room and its simplicity.

There was a ping-pong table against the far wall, adjacent to what looked to be a bookshelf but was severely lacking in actual books. On the other side of the room was a pool table.

Besides the games, it was a rather unremarkable room. Ugly almost, compared to the rest of the resort. The walls were painted a light blue that clashed with the dark blue of the carpeting. I wondered which designer decorated this room - and had no doubt been fired because of it. Why was it even still here?

"Air hockey?" I asked, my disbelief evident. When he ignored me yet again, I leveled a glare at him. "Are we playing?"

He gave me a look that made me question my sanity. Geez. It was just a question.

He bent over to put quarters into the machine, and I took the time to shamelessly admire his butt. I honestly hadn't meant to at first, but it had been right in front of me (ha ha. But. Get it?). Realizing what I was doing, I focused instead on the peeling wallpaper at the very top of the walls. Declan wasn't a person to be objectified. I hated when it was done to me, so why would it be any different for him?

"I'm sorry," I blurted when he turned towards me. He

raised an eyebrow in question. "For staring. At you. When you were bent over."

When he just continued to look at me strangely, I signed, "your butt."

I expected him to be mad, I would've been, but he surprised me by doubling over in hysterical laughter. I had seen the other guys laugh, and I had even caught a smile gracing Declan's hardened features, but I had never seen him outright laugh before. It did funny things to me.

"What's so funny?" I demanded. "Aren't you pissed that I checked out your...you know."

Of course, that only made the idiot laugh harder. Tears dripped down his cheeks, and he held his stomach with one hand. Huffing, I crossed my arms over my chest and waited for him to regain control of himself.

After what felt like hours, the laughter diminished from his eyes to be replaced with what looked like respect. I rationalized that I must've seen it wrong. Who would respect someone as pathetic as me?

"I'm not upset that you checked me out," Declan signed. "I'm flattered." He paused his movements, head tilted to the side as he regarded me curiously. "But thank you for apologizing though. Most wouldn't have."

I snorted. "I just didn't want to give you a double standard. I just know that I hate when it's done to me."

His eyes clouded over with an undefinable emotion before he quickly nodded to the game. The puck was already sliding across the table.

"I'll have you know that I'm the Stanley Cup winner of air hockey, so don't cry too hard when I whoop your ass," I said, grabbing the...handle? Fetus hockey stick? Guard thingy? I mean really, who actually knows the name of the thing you hit the puck with?

He placed his prong - because that was totally what I was

going to call it - on the edge of the table so he could sign
to me.

"You talk a big game. Let's see if you can back it up."

In answer, I made an exaggerated show of cracking my
knuckles.

I managed to score once. I would like to blame my loss on
my injuries, but the truth was, I sucked, and Declan was a
freaking beast. He countered every one of my moves with a
ninja one of his own. The only way I managed to score that
one point was tackling him to the ground and slipping the
puck in manually.

I was breathless from laughter by the time we finished the
fourth game. I didn't know where Declan got all those quarters, but I was grateful. I didn't realize how much I had
needed the distraction. It was dangerous for me to be alone
with my thoughts.

Smirking, I pointed a finger at his chest. "The only reason
you won was because I'm rusty. If we played another game, I
would totally kick your ass."

"So how about one more game?" he asked, calling me out
on my bluff. I feigned a dramatic yawn.

"I would, but I'm exhausted. Letting you win took a lot
out of me."

Rolling his eyes, he plopped himself onto the table, feet
dangling. He gestured for the spot beside him, and I eyed the
table with distrust.

"Are you sure it will hold my weight? According to Callie,
I need to slow down on the food." Which would never
happen because food was the only thing that gave me joy.

Declan rolled his eyes at me yet again. Sighing, I sat
beside him.

We remained silent for a few moments, both of us
watching our feet swing back and forth. It wasn't uncomfortable, which surprised me greatly. This was Declan, after all,

who seemed to hate me from the second he laid eyes on me. Maybe he had been on a guy period or whatever and was PMSing.

He finally tapped my shoulder to garner my attention, and I turned towards him expectantly.

"What happened?" he questioned. It felt more like a request than a demand. He was giving me the choice to answer him or not.

He was a stranger, yes, but I had been alone for so long that his sudden display of kindness left me confused. I craved more of it. If that required honesty, then I would give it to him willingly.

"My dad," I admitted softly. "Being a dick." I rubbed at my cheekbone almost absently, the pain from his hit only moderate when compared to the rest of my body. Declan didn't interrupt me as I did an assessment of my body. He just watched me with those wide, impassive eyes: seeing everything, but giving nothing away.

"He blamed me for Buttlicker's death," I said, barely even processing my inadvertent use of his nickname. Declan seemed to know who I was talking about though, and he didn't ask for clarification. "So he hit me. I don't know. Maybe I deserved it after what I did-"

Now he did interrupt me, an erratic flurry of hand gestures.

"No. Don't say things like that. You don't deserve this. No one deserves this type of treatment, and don't for one second believe that you are worth less than what you actually are."

His words brought tears to my eyes.

"My worth," I scoffed. "What type of worth can someone like me have? I have done so many horrible things to good people. My own parents don't even love me."

I paused, a ragged gasp escaping my throat unbidden. I

pressed my palm to my eyes to retain some dignity, but the sob escaped free.

"Why don't my parents love me?" I asked, the question haunting me. "What did I do wrong? Am I not deserving of love? Am I being punished? Because I'm sorry for anything I may have done to deserve this." The tears came down faster, blurring my vision. Of course, that display of weakness only made me cry harder. I was pathetic.

I felt Declan's arm around my shoulder a second before he gently pressed me to his chest. His touch was light enough that I knew I could get away if I wanted to. He made sure I knew it was my choice with him. Always my choice.

He allowed me to wet his shirt for who knows how long. By the time my sobbing subsided, my head was pounding, and my body felt drained.

I pulled my head up so he could read my lips.

"I'm sorry for slobbering all over you. Usually I'm not so needy and emotional. God, I don't know what the hell is wrong with me." I covered my face with my hands, embarrassed by my mental breakdown.

Declan grabbed both of my wrists and tentatively pulled them away from my flushed face. He waited until my entire focus was on him before he signed.

"No person should have to deal with what you deal with. It's okay to cry once in a while, and it's okay to ask for help. I'm sorry that you have been alone for this long, but I promise that's going to change. Your parents are assholes if they don't see how amazing you are. They don't deserve your love. Besides, my group already adopted you. Those guys are practically my brothers, and we protect our own."

I smiled at the familiarity behind those words. Our own. I liked the sound of that. Hey, if they were stupid enough to take on a crazy, emotional teenage girl, then who was I to stop them? I craved the companionship they offered. Was it stupid? Potentially dangerous to trust a bunch of strangers? Maybe.

But they were offering me friendship, nothing more. Sure, the friendship probably wouldn't last when they realized how fucked up I truly was, but I would enjoy it while it lasted.

"So, I'll be like your sister?" I asked. For some reason, Declan looked horrified by that proclamation. Maybe I had misunderstood him. Maybe he didn't want to be my friend after all.

"No! Not a sister! But a friend that we look after and protect and keep away from other boys."

"So a sister?" He was making zero sense.

"Not a sister," he insisted. "And stop saying that."

"But we're going to be friends?" I asked softly, peeking up at him through my fringe of lashes. His smile was marvelous and slightly familiar. I could lose myself in a smile like that.

"Tomorrow, the guys and I are hitting the slopes. I would like to cordially invite you to join us."

I giggled. "Well, how could I say no to a cordial invitation?"

He smiled back.

"Meet us in the lobby at 8 tomorrow morning. And dress warm."

CHAPTER 8

I arrived at 7, like the over-eager dumbass I was. Of course, that meant I had to sit around awkwardly in the lobby until the boys arrived, making small talk with the bellhop.

Jared always came over to talk to me. No matter where I was, what I was doing, or who I was with, he would find an excuse to sidle up beside me and start up a conversation.

I wouldn't consider him a friend, more of an acquaintance, but he seemed to want to become closer. If anything, he always asked me to go out to dinner with him.

Was that how friendships began? Should I take him up on his offer now that I was branching out, putting myself out there? Joining the whole "friend world"?

A growl interrupted my musings. A literal growl.

Jared looked up, startled, at the hulking figure towering over us.

I let out a heavy sigh.

"Hello, Callie dearest. What can I do for you?"

He grunted something unintelligible, continuing to glare daggers at Jared. The bellboy noticeably gulped.

Huh. Did Calax not want me to make more friends?

"Jared was just asking me if I wanted to go to dinner with him," I explained, remembering how only yesterday I attended lunch with him and his friends. Friends go to restaurants together, right?

So why did Calax look as if he couldn't decide if he wanted to vomit or punch Jared?

As if he felt my gaze on him, Calax turned towards me with a resigned expression.

"Do you want to go out with him?" he asked.

Huh?

"Well, I decided I needed to do the whole friendship thing. You know, friendship bracelets and the whole shebang. That's how I became friends with you guys...through food. Or, at least, the rest of the guys. You're still my nemesis."

Both Jared and Calax appeared confused by my answer.

"Yes, but what he's asking is if you want to go to dinner as more than friends," Calax explained, which, in turn, made *me* confused.

"Like as a sister? Because Declan made it clear last night that I couldn't be your guys' sister."

At my confession, Calax snorted, the grumpy expression left his face, replaced with amusement.

"Princess!" A deep voice called from behind me. Before I could turn around, I was picked up and spun in a circle.

"Put me down!" I said, laughing. Ronan obediently placed me on my feet, eyes surveying my face. They darkened as they took in the bruises, significantly worse than they were yesterday. Gratefully, he didn't say anything, only brushed his thumb along my cheekbone. I imagined Declan had told them everything. I wasn't mad, mainly because I would've told any of the guys if they had asked. Friendship included trust after all. Besides, it was only a body. And bodies were made to be broken and healed.

"Hello, Kitten," Ryder said, shifting his body to maneuver between me and Ronan. Ronan glared but backed away. "Did you dream about me?"

"Oh yeah. Woke up screaming too. Worst nightmare I had in months."

"That's my girl." He gave me a side hug, then allowed Asher to pull me away.

His words were quiet, meant only for me. "How are you feeling?"

"A little sore," I whispered back. "But I took some painkillers this morning, and they're starting to kick in." My arms were red and splotchy, the residual scarring of third degree burns. Not horrible. The bruises looked worse than what they were.

He nodded his head and gave me a stern look.

"Let us know if you need to take a break, or if we're moving too fast. I don't want you to feel that you need to hide your pain from us. We want you comfortable."

"I know, Ashy," I said, pinching his cheeks. He swatted my hand away, but a dusting of pink appeared on his cheek-bones. It still pleased me that I could embarrass Mr. Gorgeous.

Declan gave me a nod in greeting, and Tam muttered a "hey" before looking down. I really wanted to learn more about the shy boy. He was the same person who had spoken so dogmati-cally when he thought I wasn't listening. Who *was* Tamson...?

"Excuse me, Tam?" He glanced up, shocked at being addressed directly. "What's your last name?"

"My what?"

"Your last name."

He gaped at me as if he didn't know how to respond to

the simple question. Seriously, these boys were so strange at times.

"Uh...Jameston," he admitted at last. Smiling triumphantly, I turned back to my inner musings.

Who was Tamson Jameston?

"Sweetheart," Asher said. "You said that aloud."

I risked a glance at Tamson to see the boy blushing furiously. Oops.

"I'm sorry," I said to Tam. "I didn't mean to embarrass you."

"It's okay," he mumbled, but the red refused to leave his cheeks. I felt awful. I'm not an expert, but I'm pretty sure embarrassing someone isn't the best way to begin a friendship. Tamson seemed so innocent compared to Asher, so naive.

"Who's your friend?" Ryder asked. I turned to see his eyes zeroed in on Jared. The poor boy looked as if he wanted to shit his pants at the attention. I didn't blame him. The guys were big.

"He was asking our Addie out for dinner," Calax said, smirking. "She was debating on whether or not she should say yes. After all, our friendship started with food."

I couldn't understand what they found so funny. Did we or did we not eat food (well, order food before the stupid earthquake) to begin this unconventional relationship?

"She wants to become his sister," Calax continued.

Ryder was grinning ear to ear now.

"Was that what you intended?" he asked the smaller boy. "For her to become like your sister?"

Ronan barked a laugh, though he tried to conceal it with his hand. I elbowed him in the stomach, and he flicked my head in retaliation.

"I just thought it would be a good idea to make some new

friends, especially since Declan said I can't be the sister to your group of brothers," I snapped, offended.

All the boys began chuckling now. Even Tam had a slight smile on his face.

"Is that why you asked her to dinner?" Ronan asked Jared. "For the friendship?"

I really didn't understand why it was so funny.

Laugh it up, bastards. Laugh it up.

Asher turned towards me, a brilliant smile lighting his face.

"I love it when you speak your thoughts. It's entertaining."

"Well, right now my thoughts are saying that you guys are all assholes!"

"At least that's better than being your brother," Ryder said, chuckling. Without sparing Jared a second glance, he stepped in front of him, effectively excluding him from the conversation.

Well that was rude.

"We're sorry, sweetheart. We're not trying to be rude. It's just kind of funny...okay, look. The boy isn't asking you out to become your brother, you do realize that, right?"   Asher said.

When I looked at him blankly, he offered me a soft smile. "He's asking you out on a date. You know, like a boy and a girl going out, getting to know one another, then maybe becoming boyfriend and girlfriend."

He was...? Oh.

Oh.

I felt like such an idiot.

"If you like him like that, then ignore these big assholes and go on a date with him," Asher continued, ignoring the grumbling his assertion created. "If you don't, it's best not to lead him on."

Well that was a no brainer. I didn't date. Ever. Jared was sweet and all, and he might be considered handsome by some, but he wasn't for me. Even if I did decide I wanted to date, he didn't cause my heart to pound inside of my chest or my hands to sweat with nerves. We didn't talk naturally with one another, and he didn't cause butterflies to flutter throughout my stomach. I may be oblivious, but I knew what I felt for him wasn't strong enough to take that leap. Hell, I had even been wavering on whether I wanted to be his friend.

My answer must've been evident on my face, because Jared walked away without allowing me to explain. It made me feel like shit.

"It's better you let him know now," Asher reassured me.

A new thought occurred to me, and I glanced at the boys with wide-eyes.

"Does that mean we're on a date?"

Calax's eyes seemed to bulge out of his head. The rest of the guys looked equally perplexed.

"Huh?" Ronan finally said.

"Well, I'm a girl, and you guys are guys. We're hanging out, getting to know one another. And Declan already said I couldn't be your sister."

It made perfect sense in my mind.

"What? I...um..." Ryder sputtered. It almost looked as if he was blushing. "Let's go to the slopes!"

Before I could question his odd behavior, Declan and Calax each reached for one of my hands and practically dragged me out the door.

～

"DON'T TELL me you're afraid of heights?" Ryder taunted as the ski lift propelled us over the gleaming mountaintop. The snow glistened in the waning sunlight like tiny diamonds. It was glorious.

"Don't try to project your insecurities onto me," I huffed, shoving at his shoulder. The lift rocked unsteadily with the movement, and I laughed when Ryder's face paled.

He quickly schooled his expression.

"You're the one who didn't want to ride up," he countered. I had no argument for that, he was right. Granted, my reasons were different than what he assumed, but it was true that I had argued profusely against taking the ski lift.

Why couldn't we stay on the ground like normal humans?

"I'm not scared of heights," I insisted again.

"Whatever you say, Kitten."

Smirking, I unclenched my hand that held a previously made snowball and pelted him in the face. I had the pleasure of seeing his expression turn incredulous as he glanced from me to the melted snowball that now dripped down his chin, and back to me again.

I nearly died of laughter.

All at once, his expression sharpened with something I would almost refer to as wicked. A devious smile stretched across his face.

"Revenge, my little kitten. Karma's a bitch."

"Oh, I'm so scared," I mocked. "I'm shaking in my winter boots."

He continued to smile at me, and I knew that death was coming for me. It was so worth it.

The swaying cart stopped at the top of the mountain, and an overly helpful attendant practically carried me off. He must've recognized me as the owner's daughter. At the very least, the other skiers did not get offered foot massages.

Ryder was shaking with laughter by the time I politely excused myself from the enthusiastic young man.

"Don't even," I snapped as soon as he opened his mouth. I leaned against a wood pillar, my puffy coat restricting my arm movements. I meant to cross them over my chest, but I settled for awkwardly placing my hands in my armpits when I realized the coat wouldn't extend further. Ryder noticed my dilemma and nearly fell over in laughter.

Good. I hope he falls down the mountain and lands on his head.

I continued to glare at him as the rest of the boys arrived. My eyes flicked towards Tam immediately, noting his skin was tinged with a grayish sheen. I winced in sympathy.

"What's so funny?" Ronan asked, sidling up beside me and linking our arms. The movement was awkward, for our long skis prevented us from getting too close together.

"Ryder's being a dick," I said simply. When Ryder chuckled, I reached down, grabbed a snowball, and threw it at his face. The impact took him by surprise - though, really, he should've expected that from me by now - and he stumbled over his skis. I smiled in satisfaction as he collapsed in an undignified heap onto the snow.

"Aww. Did little Ryder fall over his little skis?" I cooed in a baby voice.

"You do realize that I have to get you back twice now. To keep things even, of course. Don't think because you're a girl I'm going to go easy on you."

"I'm all about equality," I sang. "I would like to see you try and take me down...RyRy."

His expression froze at the nickname, and Ronan snorted beside me. Calax flashed me a tiny grin, though he was eyeing his friend with an unreadable expression.

Ryder staggered to his feet, and I was only slightly disappointed when he didn't fall back down.

"I'll have you know-"

"Ryder!" a familiar voice screeched. Dear lord, that voice

sounded like a dying bird giving anal while simultaneously taking a shit.

It took me a moment to remember the name that belonged with the voice, though my mental self often compared myself to her. And found me lacking.

Elena.

Looking as fresh and perky as she had before at my pool.

With her damn fake tits...

"You seem to have an unhealthy obsession with her breasts," Asher whispered from beside me. "Care to fill me in?"

He spoke softly enough that the other boys were oblivious to our conversation. Their eyes were instead fixated on Elena with varying degrees of annoyance.

"She makes me feel self-conscious," I whispered back, my hands instinctively touching one of my boobs. "Do you think I have nice tits?"

Asher groaned, pink smearing his cheekbones.

"Sweetheart, that is one question you cannot ask a man."

"But I thought we were friends?" I said, confused. "And friends talk about boobs and periods and stuff like that. Don't bother denying it. I saw it on Netflix."

Asher let out a pained grunt.

"That's not the way it works."

Ugh. I was already failing at the whole friendship thing. Note to self: don't talk about vaginas and boobs around males. Apparently, that's a no-no conversation.

"I just wanted to check on my boys after the earthquake. Are you guys all okay?" Elena asked, eyes flashing from face to face with something akin to worry. Declan rolled his eyes, but it was Ronan who spoke.

"We're fine, Elena. And we're not your guys."

Her guys? Hmmm. Interesting.

Her face fell marginally before it was quickly replaced by a gorgeous smile.

"Okay, well, I just wanted to check up on you and remind you that my room is only a couple doors down." Her voice dropped, going quiet. "I miss you guys."

When none of the boys responded, Elena's face fell once again. It was then that she noticed me, dressed in my marshmallow suit behind Calax's broad shoulder. I lifted a hand that held one of the ski poles in an awkward wave. She glared back at me.

Rude.

"I see you have a new whore to share between you," she snapped. Calax's shoulders turned tense in front of me, and I bristled.

"I'll have you know that I am not a whore. I am their sister that isn't really a sister but a friend that apparently can't talk about boobs and vaginas. I think that makes me a...brother? Well, I would make a horrible brother, so they probably don't want me to be that either. Maybe I can-"

Declan's hand covering my mouth interrupted me. Apparently, Elena had left in the midst of my rant.

Wouldn't even let me finish my sentence. So rude.

"Sooo..." I drawled in my cutesy voice. "What was that about?"

The boys glanced at one another, blushed, and then immediately began discussing which hill they were going to conquer.

"Oh, hell no!" I said, laughing. "We are so having this conversation."

When the idiots refused to look at me, understanding clicked into place.

"Holy shit! Did you guys share her?"

Numerous shhhs were the response to my question.

"You did, didn't you? Was it serious? Did you have a calendar? This is freaking hilarious!"

"No!" Ryder hissed. "I mean, yes, but no. It wasn't a relationship or anything. It was just..."

"Sex?" I offered, pleased when the Great Ryder turned flaming red.

"Look," Ronan cut in, "she was one of the girls we had...relations with."

"One?" I said. "You shared more than one?"

I was probably more intrigued than I should've been. But, hey, weren't friends supposed to be interested in the relationship of their other friends? Maybe this could be my redeemer for the whole boob thing with Asher.

"We wanted multiple partners so we didn't get attached," Declan signed. "And so they wouldn't get attached to us."

"Did it work?"

"Obviously not with Elena," Asher said with a smirk. "She fell in love with those idiots but was too blind to see the feeling was only one-sided. She thought she could be the one to tame the beasts, so to speak. To make the wild boys settle down."

I felt a pang of sympathy for Elena. Not empathy, for I have never been in love, but a deep sense of kinship with the girl. How awful would it be to love someone and to know that they wouldn't love you back?

"Did you all share her?" I asked, glancing from face to face. From Calax's brooding expression, Declan's impassive one, Ryder's sultry grin, the twinkle in Ronan's eyes, the blush permanently staining Tam's face, to Asher's amused smirk.

"It started off with just Ryder, Tam, and me," Ronan admitted, somewhat reluctantly. My eyes widened in shock. Ronan and Ryder, I could expect, but Tam?

Apparently, the shy boy had a kinky side.

"Asher, as I said before, is our sweet, pure prince. He never wanted to involve himself in such activities with us peasants," Ryder added. He didn't sound as embarrassed anymore, as if he understood I wasn't judging him.

"Calax, of course, set his sights on only one girl," Ronan said, spiking my curiosity. Who was the mysterious girl that could capture the giant man's attention? "And Declan only joined the...*rotation*....after he broke up with his girlfriend."

I turned towards the man in question after hearing that. It was time for me to put my friend-cap on and kick some ass. Or save some ass. Or get him some ass. It was time for me to behave like a guy...like a sister that wasn't a sister but wasn't a brother. I could be a guy, couldn't I? All angst and broody and shit. And what did guys do in this type of situation? Threaten.

"Is it the whole 'that bitch, how dare she' type of scenario, or was the breakup amicable? Do I need to drive to her house, serenade her, and hand-feed her chocolates for you to win her back? Because I totally will. Just let me know if I need to bitch slap a hoe, bury a body, or write a two-hour musical."

The boys stared at me in a stunned silence before Ronan put his arm around me.

"Oh, Addie, everybody needs someone like you in their life."

CHAPTER 9

*T*he resort looked...small.

From my perch on top of the steep hill, the once magnificent building appeared rather dingy and insignificant. Even the people hustling to and from the various structures resembled nothing more than ants. Faces blended together, colors appeared muted, and words were inarticulate.

Was that all I was? Something so small and insignificant that, from afar, I was barely noticeable?

"What are you thinking about?" Calax grunted from beside me. He looked intimidating in his black winter coat and black hat. He had always been enormous, but, with the added fluff, he looked particularly terrifying. I wanted to point out that he resembled a burnt marshmallow, but I figured that I liked my limbs intact. The metal bulb in his eyebrow glinted in the sunlight.

"About the apparent insignificancy of our lives. How we're just one of billions of people attempting to put our mark on the world. How, in a couple of hundreds of years, we're all going to be forgotten."

Ryder let out a low whistle from behind me.

"Damn girl, and here I was, just thinking about what we're going to eat for lunch."

I snorted and turned towards the immense slope. It looked especially menacing from this angle, though I suppose that was the point with a name like Death Cross. I could see a few tire tracks in the snow despite the early hour. One of them appeared to swivel off course and into a tree.

Ouch.

Turning my back to the hill, I watched the guys discuss turns. I had gone down that slope hundreds of times before. Hell, I even invented an original pathway (through two trees, over a precariously positioned rock, and a sharp turn to avoid face planting into an icy river). But...

"I'm going to the bunny slope," I declared, referring to a diminutive hill a short ski away. The slope was designed for children and beginners.

The boys' faces showed disbelief.

"Don't be a chicken, Addie," Calax said.

"Come on! It'll be fun!" Ryder pleaded.

I rolled my eyes at their antics.

"Since Tam's my current favorite, he gets to accompany me."

That, of course, set off a chorus of rejections.

"Don't argue with me," I said, skiing towards Tamson and linking my arm with his. He wavered under my added weight, nearly toppling into the snowbank. I immediately released him.

"We'll meet you back at the lobby in an hour! And then you boys can buy your sister that isn't a sister some coffee!"

The boys chuckled and waved me away, though they all seemed slightly disappointed.

I skied alongside Tam in silence, arriving at the small hill situated nearby a cluster of trees. With this positioning, you had to ski through the forest to arrive at the hill, but it also assured the skier that she wouldn't hit any trees when descending.

"Um...Addie?" Tam asked. I turned to smile at him, pushing with my sticks (because I never learned the actual name of them) to glide down the hill. The movement felt natural, an extension of my own feet.

Upon reaching the bottom of the hill, I smiled up at Tam with contentment. He remained at the top, hands clenched over his own poles as he surveyed me.

Moving my skis into a V, I climbed back up the hill and skied towards Tam.

"You're obviously not a novice," Tam pointed out. "So why didn't you want to ski down the big hill with the others?"

I rolled my eyes.

"Because of you, of course."

"Me?" His eyes widened in disbelief.

"I saw your face when you were on the ski lift. You looked terrified. And then, when you were skiing towards the first hill, you looked more awkward than a baby penguin on steroids. No offense. Why didn't you tell your friends that you didn't know how to ski?"

He continued to stare at me with the same, incredulous expression, and I feared I had overstepped my friendship boundary. Maybe it wasn't appropriate of me to make such an assumption. Maybe I should've pushed him down the hill and made him take that leap of faith.

"Look," I said quickly. "I'm sorry if I did something I shouldn't have. You just looked scared, and I knew that you would never admit to the guys you didn't want to ski down that hill. I just didn't want you to be uncomfortable."

I shifted uneasily from ski to ski. *Gah.* Why was this apologizing thing so hard?

After a moment, Tamson shook his head with a timid smile on his face.

"I'm not mad. I'm actually grateful." He chuckled, a surprisingly seductive sound. "I guess I was too embarrassed to admit to the guys that I didn't know how to ski."

He blushed at the confession, though it could've been because of the cold. Yeah. It totally was because of the cold (said no one ever).

"Why?" I asked.

"Why what?"

"Why would you be embarrassed?"

At that, an almost exasperated expression contorted his features.

"Because they're...them. And I'm me."

"And?"

"They're all charming and athletic and outgoing," he admitted, his tone bitter. "And I'm not."

I let out a sigh.

"Why does it matter what they are? You don't have to pretend to be something you're not to remain their friend. Is that what this is about? You're afraid that you're going to lose them as friends?"

Tam's cheeks grew as red as his coat, and he plopped himself on the ground. His skis stuck out in an unnatural angle in front of him.

"No. I mean, I know they wouldn't ditch me. But...it's hard, you know? Hating who you are."

I sat down beside him, maneuvering my skis so I didn't stab him in the eyet. Without speaking, I unhooked my boots from the skis and then reached for his with a question in my eyes. He nodded in answer, and I began to remove his own skis.

"I understand why you said what you said, but you're wrong though." I removed his left ski, gently setting it to the side, before crossing over his legs to detach the right one.

"Just because you're not into the same things as your friends doesn't make you wrong or less than. Just different. I don't know you that well, Tam, but from what I see, you're a pretty great guy."

Tam's eyes remained fixed on his zipper as he began to fidget with it. Zip up. Zip down. Zip up. Zip down.

"Tell me, what do you like to do?"

He ducked his head down, that adorable blush rising to his cheeks yet again.

"I like to read."

I smiled conspiratorially. "So do I."

"And play video games."

"So do I."

"And..." he trailed off abruptly, and I nudged him with my shoulder.

"Don't be embarrassed. You can tell me."

"I like MMA."

"Mixed martial arts?" I asked in disbelief. I surveyed his lanky form, hidden behind layers of clothing, to his arresting green eyes. I wouldn't have pegged him for a fighter, but, then again, how much did I really know about any of the boys? Even Calax, my enemy for numerous years?

I knew absolutely nothing about MMA fighting, but I decided, right then and there, that I would research everything I could about the sport.

"Are you good?" I asked eagerly. Now that he admitted it, I could totally see him kicking ass. Oh yeah. My little Tam had a fire in him.

Cheeks burning, Tam muttered, "I'm okay."

"Do you compete in comps?" I asked.

"I used to. I stopped after arriving at Highwood Prep."

"Why?" Before Tamson could respond, a snowball materialized out of nowhere and hit me in the face. I winced at the cold sting, and Tam jumped to his feet to protect me.

Of course, I didn't need his protection, especially since I recognized that semi-hysterical laughter.

"You know I'm just going to get you back RyRy," I said, turning towards the snowball perpetrator. He smoothly skied out of the forest, Declan right behind him.

"You can't get me back for me getting you back," he protested.

"Addie can do whatever she wants to do," Asher pointed out. "And if that means revenge, then more power to her."

I smirked as the boys approached.

"Maybe I'll get Calax to hold you down while I attack you. I wonder how long it would take you to become hypothermic."

Calax chuckled, and Ryder pouted.

"No fair! He's too heavy."

I gasped in mock outrage.

"Callie! I think Ryder just called you fat. That deserves a solid sitting on, don't you think?"

"If it's you sitting on me, I think we have a deal." Ryder waggled his eyebrows suggestively at me. Apparently, those were the words that unleashed the beast. Calax lunged towards Ryder.

"Wait!" I screamed, and the boys all froze, Ryder cowering and Calax in mid-step. Once I was sure I had their attention, I gestured towards their feet. "At least take the skis off. My god, if we're going to fight, we at least should be classy about it."

The boys exchanged a glance, shrugged, and all began removing their skis, tossing them to the side.

Chaos erupted. Calax tackled Ryder, and Ronan leaped forward to help his fallen comrade. I was beginning to realize that R squared were almost always a team.

Declan joined the fray by jumping on top of Ronan and pelting him in the face with snowballs.

Asher and Tam both stayed beside me, one on either side.

"Those boys are crazy," I mused, watching Ryder shove Calax's face repeatedly into a mound of snow.

Tam and Asher exchanged mischievous grins.

"At least they're not fighting with actual bullets this time," Asher pointed out.

"That's actually a good idea!" I said, jumping up and down. "Not the bullets thing, but the shooting each other part."

"I never said anything-"

"We should go paintballing!" I squealed. My voice was loud enough to garner the attention of the four boys tangled up in the snow - and not the sexy tangled up either, though that would've been really hot.

Bad Addie. Bad.

"Have you ever gone?" Ronan asked, shaking snow out of his hair.

"Nope," I said, popping the P. "But I want to! And the teams can be all of us versus Calax!"

"Hey!" The giant in question snapped, gaze scathing. I noticed that he had a small bruise on his cheekbone, and I instinctively stepped forward to brush my gloved hand against it. He shivered under my touch.

"Are you cold?" I asked, concerned. He was two-hundred pounds of pure muscle, wearing a bulky coat and even bulkier gloves. How could a man like him be cold?

Surprisingly, it was Asher that snorted from behind me.

"He's not cold, Sweetheart."

"Shut the fuck up, Ashley!"

"Language, Callie!"

I pinched Calax's cheek, and he smiled at me sheepishly.

"What are you idiots doing here, anyway? Too chicken to go down the Devil's Anal?" I directed that last taunt at Ryder.

"For one, I'm pretty sure that's not the name, though I do like your name better. Secondly, we all agreed that we much rather hang out with you than the snobs over at the hill. Nobody can compare to your beauty." He practically sang the last line, his lilting voice causing goosebumps to erupt over my arms.

Rolling my eyes, I stuck my tongue out at him.

"You're still so fucking cheesy, RyRy."

"Admit it. It's endearing."

"In the want-to-stab-you-in-the-nuts kind of way," I muttered. Turning towards the rest of the boys, I clapped my hands together in glee. I probably looked like a young schoolgirl instigating a game of tag on the playground, but damn it, I was excited. I had never had people want to spend time with me, much less go out of their way for it. The feeling was exhilarating.

"What are we standing around for? Get your damn skis on, and let's have an adventure!"

By the time we made it back to the lodge, we were covered in sweat, dirt, and water from melted snow. Ryder, the bastard, felt the need to sit on me while pouring snow down my jacket. Calax intervened, and now Ryder was huddled near the fire, teeth chattering as he cursed me and my family.

"Damn it, woman! My balls are going to fall off! They're blue! How am I supposed to function with blue balls! They're little ball icicles now!"

My legs curled up underneath me, I rolled my eyes at Ryder's usual theatrics.

"Why am I getting the blame? I believe it was Callie that did the ball bluing."

Asher's face turned deep in thought.

"That sounded really sexual."

"Shut up, Ashy!" Ryder snapped. It seemed as if the boys were adopting my nicknames - at least the ones I said aloud. I don't know how I would feel if they knew I referred to them as Gorgeous or Sexy or Grumpy in my head. "But shit, Addie! Don't rile Calax up like that!"

"You're fine," I said. "It's not like you're using your junk anyway."

Asher choked on his hot chocolate, and Ryder narrowed his eyes at me.

"Take that back, Kitten."

"Make me, Blue Balls."

"What the fuck did I miss?" Calax asked, reappearing from the small coffee shop inside the resort. When he saw my expression, he relinquished the second cup of coffee he had ordered into my hand. Yum. He sipped from his own cup, eyes narrowed at me over the rim. Black coffee, of course, just like his soul.

And no. I don't have a flare for dramatics. Sheesh.

"Ryder has blue balls," Asher supplied, amused.

"They've turned into icicles now," he whined.

"At least they're prime for licking," I pointed out helpfully. All of the guys froze. "What? What did I say now?"

I seriously needed a rule book: The Acceptable Words and Phrases to Use Around Your Guy Friends. Maybe they should teach a class or something.

Who needs to learn about how to find X when you can learn how not to be a dick towards one another? Or when it's apparently appropriate to say "dick" around the male population?

"Why y'all so quiet?" Ronan asked he walked up, Declan

and Tamson following behind him like silent shadows. Tamson offered me a small smile, and I accepted it greedily. I got the distinct feeling that his smiles were few and far between.

"I don't know what their deal is," I said when it became apparent none of the idiots were going to talk. Ryder, still in front of the fireplace, shifted uncomfortably. When he caught my gaze, he quickly turned his body towards the blistering flames, neck turning red.

What the-?

"Ryder was talking about how his balls were icicles, and all I said was that they were now good to lick."

Silence.

Tam's cheeks were a flaming red, though I wasn't necessarily surprised. He was almost always red. What *did* surprise me, though, was the bulge I could see in the front of his pants. In the front of all their pants.

As if...

I replayed my words in my head. Licking icicles. Was there anything dirty with that? Was that slang for the nasty?

Licking icicle balls.

Licking...balls.

Well, shit.

"Shit," I parroted. "Totally didn't mean to say that. Well, I did, but I just didn't realize how sexual it would be. Oops. Is that why you guys are all getting boners? Are you thinking about me licking your balls?"

"Damn it, Addie!" Calax growled before storming away. Declan and Ronan quickly followed him.

"Where are they going?" I asked, slightly hurt at their abrupt exit.

"They're...um...taking care of business," Asher said. He rubbed at his neck, obviously uncomfortable with this whole conversation. Of course, I knew what he meant by that - I wasn't a complete idiot, just a kind of idiot - but I wanted to tease them a while longer. Actually, I just wanted to tease Ryder. It was a shame that sweet Asher and shy Tam had to get caught in the crossfire.

"What do you mean by that?" I asked innocently.

Ryder, Asher, and Tam all exchanged a look.

"I need to, uh, go," Tam said before bolting towards the hallway. One down, two to go.

"What business?" I continued. "Like schoolwork?"

"Not that type of business, Sweetheart." Asher's voice sounded strained.

"So? Are you guys going to explain?"

Again, the two boys exchanged an unreadable expression. Ryder shook his head in desperation, and Asher's eyes went wide with panic.

"Um..."

I burst into laughter, unable to handle their stricken expressions.

"I'm just fucking with you," I said, once I was finally able to breathe. Then, in a more serious voice, I added, "They're going back out to ski, correct?"

I, once again, had the pleasure of seeing two very pale faces. When I began giggling, Ryder leaned forward to whack my arm.

"You're such a little shit!"

"Your dick's a little shit," I retorted because, yeah, I was totally original.

"What the hell?" Asher said abruptly. I turned towards him in surprise, but he wasn't looking at me. His attention was on his phone.

"What?" Ryder asked, all traces of teasing vanishing from his handsome face.

"I just got a weather alert. There's a tornado warning."

"And that's a big deal because...?" Ryder asked.

"You don't understand. There's a tornado warning *here*. Right now. Only a few miles away from this resort."

"What the hell?" I exclaimed, jumping from my seat and running to peer over his shoulder. Sure enough, the weather station detailed a tornado that had been spotted only a couple miles from our location. "How is that even possible?"

"Does it matter? We need to get low. Does the resort have a basement?"

"Yes," Asher and I answered immediately.

"It's where the employees' break room is," Asher explained.

"Here!" I reached into my pocket and grabbed a key ring. Shuffling through the numerous keys, I settled on a small bronze one. "This key can be used in the elevator to lead to the basement. Grab your friends and get down."

As I spoke, I began to shuffle away.

"What about...where the hell are you going?"

"I'm going to go door to door and get everyone to safety," I said. "And then I need to find my parents."

CHAPTER 10

"*A*ddie, wait!" Ryder reached for my arm. Not constricting, but as if he was reminding me that he was there.

"You need to get down to the basement," Asher said from my other side. I looked between the two boys with bemusement.

"I need to make sure everyone gets somewhere safe. Not a lot of people have weather alerts on their phone, and, even if they did, they wouldn't believe that a tornado is heading towards us. Hell, I barely even believe it."

As I spoke, I quickened my pace. I reached the front desk at my last word.

"Addie?" a young man, whose name constantly escaped me, asked with a raised eyebrow. He glanced between me and the two men gripping each of my arms. His eyebrows furrowed together with concern. "Are you alright?"

"There's a tornado in the area. Can you set an alarm or make an announcement to get everyone to the first floor?" I knew the safest place would be the basement - it was below ground and had numerous rooms with no windows - yet employees were the ones with the key to access that level, and only certain ones at that. I doubted even Asher had a key.

"Are you sure?" The employee asked in disbelief. I resisted the urge to slug him.

"I'm pretty damn positive based on the weather alert," I huffed. "Can you make an announcement or not?"

He still eyed me with skepticism, but he eventually nodded.

"Yeah, I can make an announcement over the intercom."

"Thank you," I said stiffly. I knew I was being a bitch, but I didn't care. Those seconds he spent arguing with me were precious seconds taken away from people finding shelter. Now how was I going to communicate with the people hitting the slopes? Hmmm...

"Now that you have that taken care of, let's go to the basement," Ryder said, grabbing my arm once again. He attempted to drag me towards the elevator, but I dug my heels into the carpet.

"What about the people outside? And the other boys? And my parents?"

"It looks as if security is handling the people outside." Asher nodded his head towards a group of men heading towards the resort's doors. They looked far too casual for the disaster that was about to occur if the tornado struck here. The bastards didn't believe me!

I was tempted to shove the phone in their snotty faces, or maybe just hit them repeatedly until they gained common sense.

"I'm not sure that's the best idea," Asher mused. "We kind of need them conscious to spread the word."

"Get out of my head!" I snapped, slightly irritated. He snorted.

"Quit speaking aloud."

Damn him and his logic.

"I texted the guys," Ryder broke in. "They're meeting us here."

"They're meeting you here," I corrected. "I need to go find my parents."

The boys both looked at me as if I was insane. Well, more insane than normal because I'm pretty sure they already knew I was a few screws short.

"Why?" Ryder sputtered.

"Because they're my parents, and they're too stupid to move without me pushing them."

And them pushing me back, I thought but didn't say.

"Why do you even bother with them?" Asher asked, voice rising with disbelief. I shrugged. I didn't quite understand it myself, so I knew it was pointless to try and explain.

"They're my parents," I admitted at last. "The egg and sperm donor that made me into being. Sure, they're emotionally and physically abusive assholes, but I wouldn't be who I am today without them."

Their faces darkened at my words, but they didn't refute my claim. Mom and Dad may not have been family, but they were blood. That had to count for something, right?

Then why did the thought of finding them make my skin crawl?

I couldn't decide if that made me a horrible person or a smart one.

We walked down the hallway, Ryder and Asher on either side of me.

"Where are the others?" I heard Ryder ask Asher.

"I told them to meet me by the elevator," he responded. "If we're not there in ten minutes, I told them just to go without us."

Ryder snorted.

"Do you think Calax will listen?"

"Not likely."

"You know," I began conversationally, sidestepping a family that was hurrying towards the staircase. "You guys don't have to come with me."

Asher smirked, and Ryder actually began to laugh. Elbowing me in the stomach gently, Ryder said, "Not happening, Kitten."

"We already said that we adopted you," Asher added.

"But not as a sister," I pointed out. The two boys exchanged a quick glance - a bro glance, I surmised. It was impossible for me to decipher.

"Not as a sister," Ryder agreed at last. We reached a fork in the hall, and I led the guys to the right, through a door, and into the kitchen.

For a moment, I stood there, stunned. This was the same kitchen that, only days before, I had been tortured in, to my utter mortification. And that was what I felt: embarrassment and something akin to shame. These, I realized, were not natural emotions one should experience when dealing with abuse. I felt sick at the direction of my thoughts. I had grown so used to the abuse, the torture, that it had become nothing but second nature. It was odd for a day to go by where I wasn't attacked, either emotionally or physically. Instead of anger or sadness that one would expect, I felt nothing but a deep sense of failure. It had been my fault; it always was, and it always would be.

Asher, behind me, let out a gruff sound. It was apparent that he, too, was remembering that day.

"Why are we here?" Ryder asked with disdain. His eyes flickered towards the stovetop, as if he was visualizing my body erupting into flames on the surface. His brow furrowed, and he quickly looked away, as if he was in physical pain.

"I think my parents had a meeting today in the dining room," I explained, taking stock of the abandoned kitchen. A pound of lettuce was left unattended on a cutting board, and smoke was beginning to curl from the oven. The crew had obviously left in a hurry.

Almost absently, I turned off the oven. The last thing we needed was a fire on top of a tornado.

"At least everyone was smart enough to leave and get to lower grounds," Asher mused, obviously coming to the same conclusion I had.

"Hopefully my parents were some of those smart people," I said, though I severely doubted it. Knowing my folks, they would be sitting in the dining room, alone, screaming for waiters that would never come. My parents were idiots. Smart idiots, but idiots. And not smart. But smart. But also kind of dumb. Could someone be a smart, dumb idiot? Or maybe a dumb smart-

"Focus Addie," Ryder chided. I mentally cursed myself. Deciding whether or not my parents were dumb or smart was not productive towards our current predicament.

"I'm trying, but I-"

My next comment was cut off by a two-hundred-pound body jumping on mine. Okay, I know what you're thinking. Again, Addie? Because, yes, I was being tackled to the ground, and no, it wasn't in a sexy kind of way. I would consider it more like the piss-your-pants-because-there's-a-guy-attacking-me way.

I screamed, lifting my hands to protect my face.

Why did this always happen to me?

I recognized the man as a chef - though I couldn't recall his name. His bulky body was visible through his tattered, blood-stained clothing. Dark veins marred his skin, as if he had some parasite crawling beneath the surface. The skin itself flapped with each of his movements, not properly connected to his bones, and his eyes glowed a vibrant red.

Before I could do anything, his body was ripped off me and pushed to the side.

"What the hell?" Ryder shouted, grappling with the heavier man. Chef screamed, a guttural sound, and tried, ineffectively, to bite at Ryder's face.

He was right. What the freaking hell?

Though Ryder was young, he was no match for the immense beast of the man. In a matter of seconds, he was pinned beneath Chef's body.

Asher rushed forward and tackled Chef, a flurry of limbs and blood.

Me? I was frozen. Nothing seemed real. An almost surreal-like haze obscured my vision. Was I dreaming? Was this a nightmare?

Between my gasps of terror, one coherent thought spliced through my horror. Save them.

Almost mechanically, my hand closed on the handle of a pan. Yes, I know, a totally badass weapon. I probably should've grabbed one of the large knives that were still by the vegetables. I mean, that would've been smarter than a dumb pan, but my thoughts weren't on "which kitchen appliance would inflict the most pain". Nope, they were merely "fuck fuckity fuck" like a normal person.

I meant to aim for Chef's head, but my short stature restricted such a movement. Instead, the pan connected with his balls. Now how, you may ask, did I mix up a man's head with his manhood? That was a very interesting question, and it had an even better answer.

Which you will hear at a later time because, currently, I was meeting the wide-eyes of Ryder from where he had released the heavier man. He was panting, leaning against the kitchen counter with sweat beading across his forehead.

"Shit, Addie," he said, wincing in sympathy. His hand instinctively moved to cover his own balls, as if he was afraid my ball-clumsiness was contagious. Did he have such little faith in me?

"It was kind of an accident," I muttered, slightly indignant. Whatever Ryder was going to say was interrupted by a rasping groan. Chef was ambling back to his feet, greasy hair matted down with blood and other unsavory substances. A pungent smell reached me as he took a step closer, hands outstretched. I raised my pan.

If that fucker wanted another swing to the penis, then I would be more than happy to deliver.

Asher came from behind Chef, arms constricting around the other man's meaty neck. Chef buckled against his weight, but Asher held firm. It reminded me, vaguely, of a bull attempting to dislodge a rider. Chef's red, piercing eyes began to slowly close, as if he was incapable of keeping them opened for a second longer. He slumped to the ground like a bag of rocks.

Asher and Ryder surrounded me immediately, each breathing heavily.

"Are you okay?" Asher asked between pants.

"I should be asking you that. All I did was hit him in the balls."

"Cheap shot," Ryder muttered, and I gave him a glare.

"Next time, I'll just allow him to eat your face off!" I was lying, obviously, but he didn't need to know that. I would never allow Ryder to lose his beautiful face. But a hand? He could survive with only one.

"We need to get down to the basement. Now," Asher said, grabbing at my arm. His fingernails dug into my sensitive flesh, but I barely even flinched. I was used to pain. I welcomed it.

"No!" I argued, wrenching my hand free. The attempt was futile, for Ryder merely grabbed my other arm and began pulling me the direction we came from. "I need to find my parents and get them to safety."

"Something strange is going on," Ryder insisted. He ignored my protests as we moved down the now abandoned hallway. I hoped that meant everybody had gotten to safety. I refused to think of the alternative.

The alternative being, hundreds upon hundreds of red eyed, black veined zombies lurking through the resort. Was that what they were? Zombies?

No, that didn't seem right. There had been something resembling coherence in Chef's gaze, as well as Buttlicker's. It was hungry, almost feral, but it had most definitely still been human. I tried to recall the latest newscast, but my mind had been more focused on the inconsistent weather than on any strange viruses.

What the living hell was happening?

"That's what I would like to know," Asher muttered. He sounded uncharacteristically tense, and his muscles were held taut. For the first time since we started this mission, I reached for his hand and tugged him to a stop.

"Hey," I said, waiting until his eyes were on me. They were dimmer than usual, a mere reflection of his usual vibrant gaze. "You have to understand that what happened with Chef wasn't your fault. He was going to kill us, and you merely defended us and yourself. Do you understand?" I didn't wait for him to answer. I understood all too well the pulls of self-pity. You could drown in it, bask in the sorrow as it formed an unbreakable barrier around you. I didn't want that for Asher. No, he was too gentle, too kind, to experience such a leaden, miserable feeling. If I could take some of the burden off his shoulders, then I would do so happily. "He's not dead, okay? He's only unconscious. He's sick, but he'll be fine. We'll send him into a doctor after the tornado dissipates, and everything will be okay."

I could tell he didn't fully believe me, but I didn't know what other words of comfort to offer him. Guilt speared my chest. It was my fault that Asher had been in the kitchen in the first place. The stubborn boy had chosen to follow me, despite my protests. If anyone should be blamed for what had happened with Chef, it should be me.

I didn't say any of that to Asher or Ryder. Instead, I gave the former's hand a squeeze and led him further down the hall, back towards the elevator.

I wasn't surprised to find the other boys waiting for us when we arrived. What were they, stupid? Why hadn't they gone downstairs?

"We were waiting for you," Declan signed in exasperation.

See? Idiots.

"We're not idiots," Calax grumbled.

Total idiots.

"Let's get down to the basement," Asher instructed. He touched my shoulder, urging me in the direction of the elevator. In retrospect, it probably wasn't the smartest idea to take an elevator when there was a tornado nearby, but we weren't thinking clearly. Could you blame us? We all just wanted to escape this hellhole as soon as possible.

Fortunately, we were able to descend to the bottom floor with minimal interruptions. I'm pretty sure someone farted in the enclosed box, and I glared at Ronan, who was nearest to me. He quickly pointed an accusing finger in Calax's direction. Calax, of course, gave me a disapproving frown as if *I* was the one that had stunk up the elevator. Poor Declan, with his keen senses, looked as if he wanted to vomit as the smell assaulted his nose. He began cussing up a storm in sign language. I tried to nonchalantly hide myself in the background. They didn't need to know that the fart was mine.

Six sets of eyes turned to stare at me with varying degrees of shock.

"You tried to blame it on me?" Ronan asked, stunned.

"Addie," Ryder tsked. "I didn't know you had it in you."

"Girls fart. Get over it."

"All that hot air has to go somewhere," Calax mused, and I gave him the finger. Jesus, you would think that they had never seen – smelt – a girl fart before. Of course, the only girl they had introduced me to was Elena, and I'm pretty sure there was only a stick up her ass. It made perfect sense that she had never pooped or farted or any of the above in her life.

The boys all chuckled, and I realized that I must've spoken my thoughts aloud. I also noticed that none of the guys contradicted my Elena theory.

Despite the brief lapse of tension, nobody spoke as we stepped out of the elevator. Calax and Ronan took point, and Declan and Ryder at my back. Asher and Tam walked on either side of me. Together, the boys formed a protective cage. Normally I would've reprimanded them for treating me like I was a fragile little girl (hello, I was a ball whacking maniac) but I was too highly strung to say anything. I enjoyed the heat their combined bodies emitted; I felt safe, for the first time in my life. It was an odd feeling to know that I had people fighting for me. I went from having no one, to have a someone. *Six* someones.

I feared that they would abandon me once they realized what a mess I was. I knew the fear was irrational, a product of my depressive childhood, but it smothered me all the same.

The basement was a large assortment of rooms. The initial one we entered consisted of nothing more than supplies: a volleyball and net for the summer months, a collection of water equipment, and broken skis in need of repair. We walked through an archway and into a break room. It held a long table, a single microwave, and a time clock. I knew for a fact the resort had two break rooms. The second one, and the one most commonly used, was on the lobby floor. Further and further we walked through the maze-like basement, leaking pipes and moist walls causing the wood to become squishy. While there were no guests this deep, I spotted a few employees curled against a wall. Good. At least some people had gotten to safety.

One of the girls I recognized as Shannon, the hostess Ryder rejected, and I gave her a small wave when our eyes met.

We finally stopped at a small room with minimal shelving and no windows. With a grunt, Calax handed me a hardcover book. He must've grabbed it from one of the other rooms. When I stared at him with a raised eyebrow, he rolled his eyes.

"To protect your head."

"I knew that." I totally didn't know that.

Calax distributed books and game board boxes to the other boys, and then gestured towards the far wall. As I watched, transfixed, the boys sat facing the peach painted wall.

"What are you guys doing?" I asked.

"Didn't you ever have a tornado drill at your school?" Ryder questioned. "You grab something hard to cover your head, you go to a room with no windows, where no shit can fall on you, and you face the wall."

I didn't bother to point out that I had never been to an actual school before.

"But why the wall? That seems dumb."

"It's to...just shut the fuck up and sit down."

I chuckled at Ryder's flustered answer, but obediently sat crossed legged beside him.

"Use the book to cover your head," Asher instructed. I frowned.

"What could possibly fall on my head?"

"Stop arguing," Calax muttered, and I couldn't help but chuckle at the giant beast of a man crouched in a fetal position with Candy Land balancing on his head. He glared at me, but a tiny smirk pulled at his lips. He found it as amusing as I did.

"So," I began conversationally. "How did your boner handling go?"

Beside me, Ryder sputtered.

"Boner handling?" he asked.

I pressed my forehead against the wall, allowing my eyes to flicker from face to face. While Ryder was on my right, Declan sat on my left. Calax was beside Declan, a crimson flush on his cheeks. I could've sworn these boys blushed more often than any girl I had ever met.

Granted, I had only met like five girls, and I was only on a first name basis with three of them (if you counted Elena, though she didn't even know my name).

"Boner," I repeated slowly, in case any of the guys were confused by the word. "You know, like when your dick-"

"We get it," Ronan said. Declan tapped my arm, and I turned my face towards him expectantly. Frowning, he raised an eyebrow at me, and I signed him our conversation.

His face paled, and he quickly turned towards the wall.

"First I'm not allowed to talk about my breasts, and now I'm not allow to mention your boners?" I asked in disbelief.

"I'm just going to point out that our little Addie has had bare minimum human interaction," Ronan said, a smirk in his voice. To me, he said, "I take it you're not the most socially capable person?"

I scoffed. "I'm socially able to talk about dicks and stuff."

"Sweetheart..." Asher groaned. "You can't just...I mean...this is...ugh. Does anyone want to take it from here?"

"No!" was the immediate response from the other five boys.

Ugh. Calax was such a dick.

"What?" The dick in question sputtered. "Why me?"

"Because you're my nemesis," I pointed out. "And I just felt like thinking of it."

There was a long pause.

"Not *your* dick," I hurried to explain, "but you *as* a dick."

"Are we ever going to hear the story of how you guys became enemies in the first place?" Asher asked. There was a laugh in his voice, and I reached over Ryder's head to slug him. I only felt moderately guilty for the action.

"Vicious," Ryder said with a smirk.

"I'm curious about that story too," Tam piped up. "What exactly happened?"

"Well," I began, stretching my taut muscles. My shirt unintentionally rode up with the movement, and I noticed both Ryder and Declan's eyes both zero in on the swath of skin exposed. Now, it was my turn to blush, and I quickly tried to compose my features into some semblance of control.

"Well?" Ryder pressed, knocking my knee with his own.

"I don't want to talk about myself anymore," I huffed. If there was one thing I didn't feel comfortable talking about, it was my first meeting with Calax. I could tell from the tightening of his features that Calax felt the same.

"Does our little princess have a secret with the big bad wolf?" Ronan cooed.

"He's more of an asshole than a wolf," I mused.

Calax grunted. "Why do you...? Okay, never mind. Moving on."

"Listen," I began hesitantly. I shifted from knee to knee, and Declan put a gentle hand on my arm to settle me. Realizing that I had his attention as well, I spoke aloud while simultaneously signing. "I'm sorry if I say stuff that is inappropriate or wrong or whatever. I have never...well....I never had friends before, guys or girls. My entire life I've had no one. Sure, I have a spine made of steel *now*, but it was forged from continuous battles I had to face alone. There was one point in my life where I was confined to my room with only my tutor as company. I don't know how to interact with people, especially guys. If I say something wrong or stupid, just tell me. My entire life experience has been from books and television..." I trailed off, suddenly feeing silly for my impromptu confession. The world should seriously invest in a manual for these types of things: Making Friends for Dummies. Did they have something I could buy off Amazon?

"We understand, Sweetheart," Asher said. "Nobody here is judging you, okay?"

"Except for maybe Calax because he's your nemesis and a bastard," pointed out Ryder smugly. I heard rather than saw said bastard hit Ryder upside the head. I couldn't help but giggle.

"I feel like you guys know everything about me, but I know nothing about you guys," I continued, desperate to steer the conversation away from my depressing childhood and into safer grounds. Friends ask friends questions about each other, right?

Then why did all the guys look uneasy?

"We don't know everything about you," Ronan pointed out. "We don't know your favorite color or your favorite animal."

"Or how you learned sign language," Tamson added softly.

"Green, but not a grass type of green but a yellowish green. Kind of like Declan's eyes," I answered, and my mind flashed to a different set of eyes. Eyes that had haunted me for years now, but also gave me strength. The eyes of someone I once loved unconditionally and who had loved me in return. Biting my lip to keep from admitting all that, I said, "and a white tiger."

"The third question?" Asher prompted.

I shrugged. "No reason, really. Boredom? That seems right. It was one of those long months where I wasn't allowed to leave my bedroom. I learned French and some Russian as well." Before the guys could assault me with more questions, I hurried to ask, "and you guys? Tell me how you became friends."

They exchanged glances, seeming slightly wary, before turning towards me. Under their combined stares, I felt suffocated, but not in a bad way. One could relish in their attention.

"We go to school together," Asher replied oh so helpfully. I rolled my eyes.

"Kind of knew that. But how did you become friends? You're all so different."

At this, Ryder chuckled.

"Is that a bad thing, Kitten?"

"Just shut up and answer the question."

"To be completely honest, we were kind of forced," Asher said with a chuckle.

"Forced?"

If I wasn't mistaken, though I usually was, that did not seem like the ideal making of any friendship. Granted, I wasn't an expert or anything, but friendship should be a natural bond between individuals, not two dolls pressed together while a child screams "kiss".

"Yeah," Ryder said, taking over the story. I was beginning to understand that Ryder liked being the center of attention. I couldn't decipher if this was because of his vanity or something else. Something deeper. Perhaps he didn't even realize he did it, like an innate need inside of him to be seen and be heard. "At our school, we are put into groups based on our talents and goals. We work with these people throughout the years. It's kind of inevitable that we would become friends."

I considered his words thoughtfully. What type of school did they go to?

"It started off with just Ashy and me," Ryder said, ignoring Asher's grumble not to call him "Ashy". "We were already friends before they paired us up."

"We lived in the same foster home," Asher explained. I lifted an eyebrow but didn't ask him to elaborate. I understood too well about pasts. The good, the bad, and the macabre. I didn't know the reasons for such a placement, and I didn't ask. They would tell me if they wanted to. The more you pressed, the further you pushed people away.

"Asher was the annoying twat that always followed me around," Ryder said with a smirk.

Asher groaned. "You were bigger than me, and I thought that meant you were cooler."

I couldn't help but laugh with the rest of the guys. Asher was adorable, even when he whined.

"I still am bigger than you, at least in the departments that matter." Ryder wiggled his eyebrows.

"Was he a pervert as a little boy?" I asked no one in particular. I couldn't help but picture a ten-year-old Ryder hoping to catch a peak underneath a woman's skirt.

"I am not a pervert," he huffed indignantly. "I just like women."

"Too much," Tam muttered.

"Back to the story!" I said, clapping my hands together. I knew there were other things I should be thinking of - like the virus or drug or whatever the hell it was, and the tornado that may or may not hit at any moment - but that all felt like a distant memory rather than reality. A nightmare. I was good at suppressing unwanted thoughts, though I knew how unhealthy that practice was. Fortunately - or was it unfortunately? - it seemed as if the guys had adopted the same defense mechanism.

"We were taught together," Ryder continued. "Worked together. Did everything together, pretty much."

"I don't understand how these groups work," I admitted. "Are they common in schools?"

"That's complicated to explain," Asher answered.

"But-" I was interrupted by the vibration of my phone. Startled, I practically leapt three feet into the air, an uncharacteristic squeak leaving my mouth. Ignoring the laughter of the guys, I pulled my phone out of my pocket. In all honesty, I had completely forgotten about it. Why would I need a phone when the only people I had to call were my parents? For the most part, the piece of technology was left unattended and forgotten in a bedroom drawer. I had grabbed it this morning on the off chance the guys wanted to exchange numbers.

Hearing it said aloud - or at least in my thoughts which were probably still aloud - made me feel pathetic.

BASTARD: Where the hell are you?

"WHO TEXTED YOU?" Declan signed, attempting to peer over my shoulder. I flicked his ear.

"Don't be a nosey shit," I said, but my attention remained focus on the phone. Damn technology and damn my father. My lips turned down in a frown.

ME: There's a tornado. I'm in the basement.

. . .

BASTARD: Come to the lobby. I need to talk to you.

THE MALICIOUS "OR ELSE" hung unwritten in the text.

"I need to go," I said, pocketing my phone.

"Why?"

"In the middle of a damned tornado?"

"Don't be stupid."

"It's my father," I said, as if that would explain everything. For me, at least, it did. No one left D.O.D. waiting.

"Screw the bastard," Ronan said.

I snorted. "Easier said than done. You're not his daughter." And you don't have to face his wrath. I didn't say those words aloud, but I could tell from the guys' frowning faces they understood the unspoken words.

"Is he trying to get you killed?" Calax exploded, his hand clenching into fists.

"Wouldn't be the first time," I muttered. Louder, I said, "I'll be right back. Besides, the tornado probably missed the resort, if it is even still, you know, tornadoing."

"Tornadoing?" Ryder asked in disbelief. He really needed to stop doing that. I didn't know how this friendship would work if he constantly questioned my word choices.

"She's right, though," Asher said quietly. "It was a tornado warning, yes, but from the weather projection, there was only a slim chance that it would hit the resort."

"Still-" Calax began, but I held up a hand to stop him.

"No, Calax. You don't get to tell me what to do. I don't need you to always protect me." I met his eyes over the top of Asher's head. In his gaze, I could see a swarm of emotions, some I couldn't entirely understand. One thing I knew for certain was that there was no hate in his gaze. I knew hate; I saw hate in the leering gaze of business partners and my parents regularly. This...I didn't know what this was, but it wasn't something I was familiar with.

"Fine," Calax said at last. With surprising agility given his immense size, he lumbered to his feet. "I'm coming with you."

"No," I hurried to respond. "My parents-"

"Your parents are no longer just your problem. They're *our* problem now. I should've come earlier, I should've realized earlier, and I didn't. That's on me. But that doesn't mean that I won't help you now. I'll be damned if I let anything happen to you when I could've prevented it."

I knew the resolve in his gaze mirrored of my own. There was no changing his mind.

"Fine, but only you. The rest of you-" I leveled my glare on the rest of the boys, "-will stay here."

Before anyone could protest, Declan nodded stiffly.

"Fine. But you better come straight back."

We exchanged a long look. I could tell that he didn't agree with my decision to only bring Calax, but he respected it. We may not have been friends, he may have hated me, but we understood each other at that moment. My decision was for my own sake as much as theirs.

I wouldn't be able to live with myself if something happened to my new friends because of me. I was already putting Calax at risk, though there was nothing I could do about that. The bastard was more stubborn than I was.

And yes, he was still a bastard, even if he did look at me as if we were lovers instead of enemies.

Even if he did want to protect me.

It was safer that way, both for him and me. I didn't do feelings or emotions; I didn't let people in. It was easier.

"Come on, Callie. Let's go see what my lovely parents want."

CHAPTER 11

I leaned my back against the fence, the ragged metal jarring the bruises on my spine. Still, I did not dare grimace or allow any outward expression of my pain. Ducky didn't - couldn't - know the truth.

"Do you have a date yet?" I asked him through the barrier that separated us. He sat directly on the other side of the fence. I could feel the fabric of his shirt against my bare arms.

I was fortunate that his school went up to eighth grade. The only other public school, the high school, was a couple miles away, and I was too lazy to walk that far.

Though, for Ducky, I would've.

"Tomorrow," Ducky answered, touching his cascade of long hair. He constantly grew his hair out, cut it, and then donated it to a foundation that made wigs for cancer patients. His mom had died of the disease when he was a young boy, and this was his way to honor her. Though his foster parents didn't necessarily agree with his decision (the teasing had escalated from taunts into fights), they left Ducky alone to do as he pleased.

I always envied his hair, both long and short. For years, I wished that my hair would grow as fast as his did. It looked like silk. With a desire that was only slightly irrational, I longed to run my fingers through it.

"So, your thirteenth birthday is coming up," Ducky said conversationally. He absently scratched a drawing into the sand with a stick. The sun, peeking through the boughs of trees, illuminated his pale hand as he drew.

At his age, they weren't allowed to have recess anymore (which I found ridiculous), so we were forced to meet up before and after school. It was difficult, what with my parents and his foster parents, but we were able to see each other at least two times a week. I would've preferred that number to be higher, but beggars couldn't be choosers or however that saying went.

"Don't remind me," I answered, rolling my eyes to the heavens. While birthdays were grand affairs for some, mine consisted of nothing but formal dinners and the occasional wandering hands of my parents' "friends". I had never received any presents from anyone other than Ducky, but I didn't mind. What could my parents possibly give me? A "I'm sorry I beat the crap out of you" t-shirt? Or a "I'm a sick bastard" coffee mug? They didn't know me, and they didn't know what I liked. I had long since accepted the hand I had been dealt.

"Are you doing anything?" he pressed.

"The usual. Dinner at Holt's, and then a long spiel about how age comes with responsibility and blah blah blah." I didn't bother to mention the beating that I was bound to receive. He didn't need to know that part. It wasn't his burden to carry.

"What time?"

"Seven."

I had thought he was only being inquisitive, as was standard with Ducky, but I should've known better. He was trying to be my friend, trying to show me something that my parents had neglected to show me for so long. Love.

And it was his love for me that would cost him his life.

THE TORNADO HIT ONLY moments before we reached the stairwell.

We were in a small room that had once been a second restaurant. A long bar was against the far wall, glasses piled in shelves behind it. A dozen tables were left abandoned in the center of the room, many collecting dust from years without use.

I remembered this room. My mother had wanted a pub and took it upon herself to hire a designer to recreate a 1930s nightclub. Apparently, Mommy dearest was having an affair with said designer, who mysteriously disappeared. Thus, the bar never came to be, and the basement as a whole had been abandoned for storage. Daddy was a vindictive son of a bitch.

For a moment, I thought that it was another earthquake. The feeling was very similar - the ground almost seemed to vibrate, and glasses from the shelf rained down upon us.

Calax reached for me, but one of the shelves came loose, and it plummeted down, hitting Calax in the head. The giant immediately dropped to the ground, blood pooling from the wound.

Ah. That was what the book was for.

I couldn't help my slightly incoherent thoughts as panic set in. I knew I couldn't stay in this room - there was broken glass everywhere, and large objects pelted me like hail. I knew all this, I did, but I couldn't leave Calax, and it was impossible for me to drag him out. I considered running back towards the guys, but I didn't want to put them in harm's way.

I did what instinct demanded: I threw myself on top of Calax. Being careful of the blood gushing from his forehead, I attempted to shield his massive body with my small one. I hoped the effort wouldn't prove futile.

Spreading my legs and arms further apart, I tucked my head into his hair to avoid the worst of the onslaught. I felt something particularly heavy hit my back, and I let out a whimper.

Breathe, Addie. Breathe.

My therapist always told me that, in any situation, all I had to do was breathe. If I was still breathing, there was a chance that everything would work out.

So I breathed. I breathed through the pain that seemed to almost consume me. I breathed when a shard of glass impaled itself in my arm, eliciting a sob from me. I breathed even when a table landed on my leg, crushing the bone.

I knew, without a doubt, that it was broken.

The pain was immediate and intense. It wasn't my first broken bone, but it was definitely one of the worse. Tiny licks of fire erupted in my veins.

Breathe. Just breathe.

Why didn't that sound appealing anymore?

After what felt like hours, the wind subsided, and the air went still.

I trembled, still sprawled overtop of Calax.

What the hell happened?

It was the middle of winter, the middle of fucking winter in Michigan, and a tornado just hit. This, along with the earthquake, was not natural.

"What the hell? Addie..."

I let out a noncommittal grunt.

"Shit! Princess!" I felt someone gently grab my arms,

pulling me off Calax and onto my back. I let out an involuntary screech as the pain in my back amplified.

Shit. Fuck. Shit. Ball sucking dick.

"What the fuck happened?" I knew that angry voice, though I don't think I had ever heard it with that particular inflection. Tam. Why was he angry?

"It looks like she threw herself on top of Calax. To protect him." Ryder sounded almost furious with that assumption.

Another hand - Declan's perhaps - repositioned me so I was on my stomach. That felt better for my back, but worst for my arm. The slab of skin that had been cut by glass was now pressed against the flooring. Shifting, I moved onto my back yet again.

Better. Not great, but tolerable. The lesser of two evils.

"Shit! Look at her," Ronan said.

"Her leg's broken," Asher pointed out.

No shit.

Someone snorted. Ryder. "At least she still has her sense of humor."

"I will always have a sense of humor," I whimpered. "Even in death." Wincing, I turned my head to see Asher now leaning over Calax. "How is he?"

"He's fine. The big glute's just unconscious for now. He's going to be pissed when he gets up though."

I tried not to let out a scream as Declan did something to my leg. I'm afraid that I made a howling noise instead because, apparently, that's so much sexier than a cry of pain.

"Why would he be angry?" I managed to gasp out. "I saved his life."

At this, the boys all exchanged amused glances.

"That may be," Asher began. He seemed to choose his words carefully. "But Calax would've preferred for you not to risk yourself for him."

I let out another sound - a laugh, perhaps? I couldn't

really tell. My mind was fuzzy, both from pain and the fact that Declan had taken his shirt off, using the material to make bandages for me. I couldn't help but appreciate the expanse of golden skin on display. If I had somehow died, at least I was in heaven.

"You're not dead," Ryder said in exasperation. "And if you think he looks good, you should see me."

Another choked laugh escaped me at that. Ryder was such a cocky bastard, but he was growing on me. Like a fungus.

I was slightly disappointed when Declan only ripped off the hem of his shirt before throwing it back over his head. Shame. A body like his deserved to be on display.

"You don't care that I was just eye fucking the shit out of your friend?" I asked, raising one eyebrow in disbelief.

"Fortunately for the both of us, he's constipated," Ryder answered with a wink. It took me a moment to understand what he said, but, when I did put it together, I threw my head back in laughter.

Luckily, Declan's attention was fixated on my injuries, so he couldn't read my lips. I had the feeling that he would either laugh at me again or turn back into Mr. Glarey. The verdict was still out on that one.

"Are all of you guys okay?" I asked. "Any injuries?"

"We're fine, Princess," Ronan said reassuringly. "You are by far in the worst shape."

"Gee, thanks. Way to make a girl feel pretty."

"Well, you're beautiful. You could never be just *pretty*."

I snorted, my standard response when it came to these men. Still so fucking cheesy.

"What else hurts?" Declan signed after he waved his hands to gain my attention. I frowned; the boys really should be checking on Calax. I was fine, more than used to the pain that seemed to emanate from every pore in my body. Pain was just that...pain. It didn't determine the severity of an injury.

"My back and arm," I admitted at last. "Some glass got stuck...and I think something landed on me."

Tam moved to my side, his tentative hands rolling up the sleeve of my shirt. They paused, at first, as they ran over the old scars from my self-inflicted injuries. A tremor went through his body before he settled on pulling out tiny shards of glass.

"Shit!" I hissed after a particularly nasty piece was removed. Yup. Glass still stung like a bitch.

Turning my head, my pulse spiked when I noted Calax's prone body. Was he breathing? Oh god, what if he was brain dead?

"He's not brain dead," Tam admonished gently. He glanced towards me, blushed, and then refocused on treating my wounds. "He's just unconscious."

"Hey, lazy bastard!" Ryder cupped his mouth to amplify the sound. He landed a light kick to Calax's stomach. "Wake up! Kitten is worried about you!"

The giant didn't even twitch. My heart hammered in my chest.

Ryder kicked Calax again. "It's Addie! Calax come quickly!"

At that, Calax's eyes snapped open. With surprising speed, he sat up, eyes casting a quick, panicked look around. They noticeably relaxed when they landed on me, only for alarm to set in when he took in my condition.

"What happened?" he asked, crawling towards me. Asher half-heartedly warned Calax against moving with his head injury, but it surprised no one when Calax ignored him. Once he was above me, a towering pillar that blocked out every other face, his expression calmed. His hand gently smoothed my blood encrusted hair.

"What happened to you, Baby?" he asked, so softly that I had to strain to hear him.

"You were unconscious," I explained. "I had to protect you."

He swallowed, his Adam's apple bobbing.

"Why would you do that?"

I didn't have an answer for that. Because we were friends? Because you were vulnerable, and I was capable of helping?

Because, for once, I wanted to save a life instead of end one?

I didn't say any of that. Instead, I just gazed up at him. His eyes looked incredibly tender. I half expected him to yell at me, call me stupid, but I only saw awe in his commanding gaze. Awe...and that other emotion that I shall not name.

I chose not to look too far into that. Another day. Another time.

"What about Shannon and the others?" I asked, breaking my gaze away from Calax's.

"Who the hell is Shannon?" Ryder questioned.

"The girl you were flirting with yesterday," I answered with a roll of my eyes. "Blond hair? Hostess at a restaurant? Only dates football players?"

"Nope. Don't remember."

I smiled through dried blood.

"You're such an asshole sometimes."

"Yes, but I'm your asshole."

"You're not my anything."

"Let's discuss this later," Asher said, not unkindly. "Addie needs to get to a hospital."

"Is it safe to use the stairs?" Tam asked. I couldn't see the state of the room, but, from their cautious expressions, I gathered it was not in the best shape. Shame. I rather liked the half-finished restaurant.

There was a shuffle of footsteps and what sounded like

chairs being scraped against the wood flooring. I wanted to crane my neck to see, but I was in too much pain.

The ceiling was much more interesting anyways. All cracks and, well, more cracks. And were those cracks inside of cracks?

"Please stop talking about cracks," Asher said. "Ronan's dirty mind is making him giggle like a schoolgirl." Said schoolgirl began to laugh harder.

"So apparently Ronan is the pervert, not Ryder. Interesting," I mused. Ryder let out a gleeful whoop while Ronan began to protest. While I listened to the boys argue, a new thought occurred to me.

How much did I really know about these guys? Sure, Ryder came across as a huge flirt, but what was he really like? And Asher, was he really the sweet, charismatic boy he appeared to be, or was there more to him?

"Um...I don't know how to respond to that," Asher mumbled, cheeks burning in my peripheral vision.

"And I am most definitely just a flirt," Ryder insisted. "No character, no substance. Just a pain in the ass."

"That's what she said," I muttered softly.

"A woman after my heart," sighed Ryder dramatically, and I snorted. I'm pretty sure he didn't think with that organ whatsoever.

"Entrances are blocked," Tam said, voice distant. I heard the shuffling of footsteps.

"What about the others down here?" I asked weakly. "Did you check on them yet?"

Ronan rolled his eyes with a huff, but there was a cheeky grin on his face.

"So needy."

I gave him the finger in response.

"Should we congregate with the others?" Calax asked

anxiously. He hadn't stopped stroking my hair since he'd awoken. I would've yelled at him if it hadn't felt so nice.

I mentally berated myself for the direction of my thoughts. I wasn't supposed to be thinking about Calax in that way. Nice wasn't a word I liked to associate with the beast of a man. Sure, he looked like a ferocious giant, what with his defined muscles, black clothing, and glowering expression, but...

But he was never like that with me. He was always so tender, as if I was precious glass he was afraid would break. Maybe that was why I classified him as public enemy number one. If I were to look at him in any other way, any other light, I would break.

For him? Because of him? Despite of him?

The world may never know.

I shifted my attention away from Calax to Tamson. As if he felt my eyes on him, Tam looked up, blushed, and then quickly glanced back down at his feet.

If there was one thing I noticed about Tamson, it was his inability to make and maintain eye-contact with me. The knowledge didn't hurt or bother me as it might've some. From what I gathered in our brief interactions, Tam was shy and often felt inadequate when compared to his friends. I didn't agree with his self-assessment, but I understood it. I had lived my entire life under a spotlight while longing to lose myself in the shadows. Every detail, every word, every action constantly analyzed in extensive detail. Despite the amount of effort I put into it, I always came up short. Lacking. I understood Tam, and his need to hide behind his curly hair. There were some points where even my hands didn't want to be seen.

So, no, I didn't judge him for his timidity. If anything, I respected him for being who he was, anxiety and all.

I was actually *grateful* when his eyes had fluttered away

from mine. I didn't want to make eye-contact with any of the boys. Calax made me feel too much, too deeply, and I understood how dangerous that could be.

"I vote yes to the whole congregating thing," I said brightly, my attention fixated on a spot above Tam's shoulder. From this angle, still on the ground, I could just make out the peeling wallpaper and exposed wood-frames. The depressing structure seemed to balance on the precarious few pillars that remained standing.

Good god. If this was the basement, how does the rest of the resort look?

"Probably not good," Asher answered solemnly.

"I just hope there aren't any casualties," I whispered. My heart hurt at the thought. I may have, at times, appeared callous when it came to death, but that was only when it involved me. It was entirely different when death concerned others. Perhaps it was selfish thinking, but I couldn't bear to witness anymore death. After Buttlicker (I really should figure out his real name), I had thought I could brave anything. After all, it was my fault he was dead. Even if I hadn't pulled the trigger, he, no doubt, was in the hospital looking for me. Did his unintentional death by my hand make me a monster, even if his intentions for seeking me out were malicious at best?

I chose not to look too closely at that answer.

"Once the fire trucks come and free us, we should gain a better understanding of what happened," Calax responded vaguely, his deep voice causing my skin to tingle. Like most things in my life, I chose to ignore the feelings that brewed inside me at the sound of his voice.

Safer. Easier.

Healthier.

"There's a bunch of people in the next room over," Asher

said from above me. He pointed over his shoulder. "Should we head over there?"

"Is it a good idea to move Calax and Addie?" Tam asked.

"Is it a good idea to stay in this room, where the walls and ceiling looks like they'll fall down on us at any moment?" Ronan countered. I didn't even have to look to know that Tam would be blushing.

Lifting myself onto my elbows, with only a slight grimace of pain (yay me!), I addressed the boys with a smile. "Would one of you gentlemen do me the honor of giving me a piggy-back ride?"

"I'll do it," Calax said instantly, and I snorted.

"You shouldn't even be walking, let alone carrying my heavy ass."

He opened his mouth to retort, no doubt against my claim of being heavy, when Ronan bent down before me.

"Hop on, Princess. Your majestic steed awaits."

"Why thank you, kind knight," I said with feigned reverence. Ryder and Asher helped position me on Ronan's back, with extra care to not disturb the bone protruding from my leg or the injuries on my back. I clung to Ronan like a monkey, arms around his neck and my good leg wrapped around his muscular torso.

I could feel my pants dropping down, and I hoped I wasn't displaying the crack Ronan liked so much.

As if he read my mind, or heard me, more than likely, Asher leaned forward to whisper in my ear.

"Coast is clear."

"I'm not flashing anyone?" I asked, wanting to clarify. Asher blushed but shook his head no.

One small relief.

The procession to the next room was slow, mainly because of my occasional whimper of pain. I tried to suppress the sound, I honestly did, but certain movements would jar my body in a way that felt like licks of fire kissing my skin. The boys would halt at the sound, trying to reassure themselves that I was alright. I tried to tell them that they didn't need to coddle me, but that only resulted in a glare from Declan and a shake of the head by Calax.

"How long do you think we're going to be in here?" Tamson asked quietly. He was currently on rear duty - which I translated to making sure my ass didn't hit the floor. It was a surprisingly difficult feat. My arms were weak, and my body ached.

I think I just needed someone to permanently stand behind me, holding my butt up so I wouldn't slide down Ronan's body. Not in a perverted way or anything, but in a completely normal and platonic, non-sisterly-

"What the hell are you thinking about?" Ronan asked me.

"My ass," I responded immediately before I could think things through. I mentally cursed myself when I heard groans mixed in with laughter. Damn it. No butts allowed in conversation, Addie. We've been over this.

"Anyway," Calax said gruffly, averting attention to him and away from me. I could've kissed him...but not in a sexual way. A friend way. A friend that wasn't a sister way.

Stop. Thinking. Addie.

"I think the School will send people as soon as they can. I guarantee you that Sarge is already here," Calax continued, ignoring my outburst.

I fixated on the way he said school, as if it was in all capital letters. What could a preppy boarding school do against a tornado?

And another thing...

"Who's Sarge?" I asked. The boys tensed around me, even Ronan, though he tried to relax his muscles after I let out an audible squeak. I could see Calax's brow furrow, which meant he was thinking.

I hoped he didn't pass out from it.

"Sarge - Sargent - is our group leader," Calax settled on at last.

"For the school?"

Another hesitation. "Yes."

"Is that his name?" I questioned. "Or his title?"

Before Calax could reply, a high-pitched squeal made my ears bleed. Okay, maybe my ears were already bleeding because of the whole tornado thing, but that sound wasn't really helping matters.

"Are you guys okay? I was so worried!"

We had entered a room where a large group huddled together. They all had pale faces, but otherwise looked unharmed. Elena, with mascara streaming down her face like onyx tears, ran through the crowd and threw her arms around Ryder.

I couldn't help but chuckle at Ryder's flabbergasted, if not slightly horrified, expression. With a practiced efficiency, Ryder disentangled himself from Elena's arms. Of course, Elena took that as permission to throw herself at Declan who did not remove himself from her gently. He cast her a glare that would've made any sane person shit their pants. Hell, I wasn't even on the receiving end of it, and I stilled trembled.

Tamson, knowing that Ronan was out of commission since he held me and that he was next, quickly ducked behind Calax.

Elena glanced at Calax, gaze slightly hungry.

Same girl. Same.

I frowned at myself.

Nope. Not the same. Because I wouldn't ever stare at Calax hungrily. Nope. Nada. I was not hungry for Calax. I had already eaten...chicken. Chicken's better than a boy.

Ronan's chuckle clued me in to the fact I had spoken aloud. Again. Calax looked oddly pleased with himself, as if my unintentional confession reinforced something he had suspected. What that was, I had no idea.

I hated Calax. Hated him.

"I see you're still with...*her*," Elena said with a false cheerfulness. Her eyes glared daggers at me. Despite the pain and the dire situation we were in (you know, the whole being trapped underground thing), I felt something akin to glee rise up in me. I had never met a mean girl before. I'd watched movies, read books, but this was my first experience with a jealous bitch.

It made me feel...well, not normal necessarily, but less like a freak.

Yes, I realized there was something wrong with me, thank you very much.

"The name's Addie," I said, attempting to wave. Of course, that led to me nearly falling on my ass, and Tam darting forward to help stabilize my clumsy body. Elena's eyes honed in on my leg around Ronan's body and Tam's hands on my hips.

"You could put her down now," Elena suggested in a snide tone, as if we were imbeciles for not thinking of that sooner. I glanced in dismay from my leg, still broken, to Elena, and then back to my leg. Nope, apparently not even mean girls could will my bones to mend themselves. Shame.

"Don't be ridiculous, Elena," Ryder snapped. Gone was the jovial, flirtatious boy I had grown so accustomed to. This boy looked almost dangerous.

I didn't believe he would actually hurt Elena, but a small pang of fear made my heart beat erratically. I had often been on the receiving end of such of tone, and for me at least, it always resulted in a beating.

"Shit, dude. Soften your voice. You're scaring, Princess," Ronan said, and Ryder's eyes shot to my face.

"Princess?" Elena questioned.

"You know I would never hurt you or Elena, right?" Ryder asked, his voice considerably softer. He looked almost scared, his normally jubilant eyes downcast. I held out my hand to him, and he took it, giving it a gentle squeeze.

"I'm sorry," I whispered, quiet enough for only him and Ronan to hear. "I know you wouldn't. It's just...hearing your voice like that..."

"Reminded you of your parents," Ryder finished for me, just as softly. His face paled. "I'm nothing like those sick bastards, you hear me?"

"I hear you."

"Does your new toy know that you used to fuck me?" Elena asked, disrupting our moment. I blinked at her in surprise. "Me and my entire team."

She gestured towards a group of girls huddled in the far corner. They all stared at our group with varying degrees of jealousy and hatred. Yup. The boys were apparently real winners in the female department.

"At the same time?" I whispered in Ronan's ear. "Like a seven-some?"

Ronan snorted in laughter, and Elena turned her glare onto him.

"No," Ronan whispered back, ignoring Elena. "Not like that." He hesitated. "But yes, all of those girls were on the rotation at the same time."

I frowned at the way he spoke so brashly about females, as if we were just commodities to go through.

"We don't think of you like that," he assured me, easily reading the tension in my body. "You're our friend."

"And Elena never was?" I found that hard to believe. Why would they pursue a relationship with someone if that person wasn't a friend? Didn't most relationships develop from a friendship?

Sighing, I glanced up from the crook of Ronan's neck to meet Elena's glare.

"Yes, I know all about your little nightly adventures with Tam, Declan, Ronan, and Ryder. This isn't show-and-tell Elena. We don't need to talk about our conquests. Now scuttle away and leave the guys alone."

Elena sputtered, face turning red. I faced her resolutely. There were far worse storms than her. I had faced thousands of them. After a moment of heavy breathing, she smiled. It was a smile you would see on a demonic child, though I would never tell her that. Why make her feel self-conscious over her bitch smile? No, it was better for everyone involved if I mocked her silently.

"And Calax," she said smugly. "You're forgetting my night-time adventures with him too."

CHAPTER 12

The air left my lungs in a whopping rush. I could scarcely believe what I had heard.

Calax? And Elena?

No, that couldn't be true. I tried to picture it, tried to picture Calax cupping Elena's face as he had done so often with mine, but the image made me a little nauseous. I told myself the turmoil of emotion raging inside of me was pity for Elena and nothing more.

Why did it feel like my chest was tightening? Why did I have the sudden, irresistible urge to claw Elena's eyes out?

I knew the name of the emotion, but I refused to accept it. No, I was not the type of person to be jealous, especially over activities Calax may or may not have partaken in. The spastic, frantic energy I felt dissipated leaving me with only confusion.

"Shut it, Elena," Calax hissed. He took a step closer to me, and Elena's smile grew. She knew she had hurt me, and she relished in it. That...that...bitch!

"Good observational skills," Ronan muttered. I pinched his cheek.

"Shush."

"Don't listen to her. She's desperate for attention," Declan signed, making me chuckle. Elena's hair whipped in her face as she turned to glare at him before turning back towards me.

"What's he saying?"

"You're so 'in love' with him, and you didn't even bother to learn sign language?" I asked, smirking. How could she not be willing? Wouldn't you do anything, cross any oceans, for the people you loved? What she felt for these boys, I realized, wasn't love but infatuation. She was like me in that aspect: clueless of what love actually was.

"Whatever." Elena rolled her eyes as if a language barrier was only a minor inconvenience in a relationship. And then she glared at me. Again. Because apparently it was my fault the boys brushed her off.

Maybe I was wrong. Maybe mean girls were not as fun as I originally thought. Didn't, in the movies, they get hit by a bus or something?

Well, I didn't see any buses barreling towards Elena.

"Hey, I know this girl!" Another pig screeched. Excuse me, 'teenage girl said'. This girl looked familiar though her name escaped me. Considering I only knew a few people, that was a surprise.

I guess she hadn't been very memorable.

Ronan snorted beneath me.

"Bikini girl," he supplied.

"One bikini or ten?" I had to ask the serious questions here. Apparently, the number of bikinis you had determined the importance of a person.

"She was the one who had ten."

"The leather one..."

"The glass one..."

"She only wears the glass one in the sunlight. So it

reflects," I murmured. "And only when she does activities and hobbies."

"Because she has interests."

The new girl, whose name I still couldn't remember, looked back and forth between the two of us, obviously unable to hear the conversation and seemed pissed by that prospect. I didn't know why her panties were in such a twist. If I remembered correctly, she had been looking for Ryder, not Ronan.

I wasn't riding Ryder currently.

Hmmm. That was both a pun and a sex joke. I had to remember to recycle that one.

"Ronan, baby, what are you doing?" Bikini asked.

Baby?

Ronan?

He was most definitely not a baby.

"Thanks, Princess," said non-baby with a wink. I rolled my eyes.

"Wasn't supposed to hear that."

"Suck it up."

I leaned forward to stick my tongue out at him, but I accidentally leaned too far and licked his neck.

Licked. His. Neck.

Okay, so I might've just tapped his neck with my tongue, but still.

Fuck.

Ronan froze beneath me, a violent tremor running through his body. I heard him make a sound in the back of his throat: a combination between a sigh and a grunt.

Maybe if I just pretended it hadn't happen...

From the looks the boys and girls gave me - shock, disbelief, hatred, and jealousy - I figured that wouldn't work.

"Whoopsies," I said sheepishly.

"What the fuck was that?" Elena screamed. Literally screamed, as if we weren't standing two feet away from her.

"Um...an accident."

"How the fuck do you accidentally lick someone?"

"Easy actually. Like, if you're walking and you mistake someone's head for ice cream. Or if you want to stick your tongue out at someone, but you trip and fall into them. There can be a lot of reasons for accidental lickings."

Calax, seeming to forget he was jealous, doubled over in laughter. Ryder and Asher were on the ground in hysterics. Even Mr. Grumpy had a small smile on his face.

Okay. It wasn't that funny.

"It really was, Princess," Ronan said with a chuckle.

Laugh it up bastards.

"What the hell is wrong with her?" Bikini asked in disbelief. She exchanged a long, measured glance with another unfamiliar girl.

As one, the boys and I answered, "A lot."

Choosing to ignore the glares I felt piercing my skin, I nudged Ronan's stomach with my good foot.

"Put me down. My arms are sore. I'm weakening..." I said the last sentence as dramatically as possible, a poor impersonation of the Wicked Witch melting. Ronan chuckled at my theatrics but obediently lowered me to the floor. Ryder and Declan moved on either side of me to position me comfortably against the wall. I hissed at the pain ghosting down my spine, but quickly tried to mask my frown when I saw Elena looking at me. I wouldn't show weakness in front of anyone, especially her.

"What even happened to her?" Elena asked. Though her tone was stiff, her eyes appeared to be almost worried. I must've looked pretty damn bad to get such a reaction from the ice queen.

"When the tornado hit, she threw herself on top of Calax,"

Ryder explained. He sounded slightly awed, as if he was describing the actions of a mythical creature and not that of an awkward girl. His eyes were warm as they grazed my face. "Had some shit fall on her."

Elena bit her lip. She seemed to be debating something, but what, I couldn't discern. After a moment, she sighed heavily and dropped to her knees beside me.

"What are you doing?" Ronan demanded. He had, at some point during Ryder's explanation, dropped to his butt next to me. His hand currently kneaded at the muscles in my neck.

"Fixing her. You want her to keep that leg, don't you?" Elena said snidely. Turning towards me, her tone softened marginally. "What hurts?"

"Besides everything?" I asked with a chuckle. "Everything."

Elena didn't smile, but she also didn't glare at me anymore. I took that as a win.

"Her leg got crushed," Calax said gruffly. "And I think some glass got stuck in her arm."

"And her back!" Tam added.

Elena nodded slowly, gaze piercing. She immediately began unwrapping the flimsy shirt-bandage Declan had constructed.

"I need something to brace her leg on. Two pieces of wood maybe? A hard cover children's book? Whatever you can find."

When nobody made any effort to move, Elena snapped her fingers impatiently in front of Ryder's face. "Now!"

He glared at her, but got up and stomped down a hallway. Asher, after a wistful glance in my direction, moved towards another.

"What about alcohol? Something to clean these wounds with?"

"The room we just came from used to be a bar," I

supplied, nodding towards the general vicinity with my head.

"I'll go," Ronan offered. Before he left, he pressed a chaste kiss to my forehead. I was too stunned to do anything but gape after him like an idiot.

What. The. Hell?

It was because I licked him, right? The whole licking incident opened up a large can of worms.

Calax, muscles bunched together as he crossed his arms, glared down at us from above. He really was an impressive man, all muscles and chiseled bones.

"I'm not going to be able to work if you're glaring down at me," Elena snapped. Her hands were tentative as they assessed my injuries. "Go wait over there."

When Calax didn't budge, Elena removed her hands from me with a sour expression.

"If you don't move, I won't fucking help her."

If looks could kill, Elena would've been dead a thousand times over. After one more ineffectual glare in her direction, Calax stormed to the corner. He leaned against the wall, eyes trained on me as if he couldn't bear to look away. The attention felt...strange. I didn't know how else to describe it. I couldn't decide if I enjoyed it or feared it. He disarmed me with his gentleness.

From the corner of my eye, I watched Declan sign to Tamson. I couldn't see the movements, but I saw Tam nod and get to his feet. Before I could inquire, Tam turned back towards me with a smile.

"I'm going to see if there's any water or something to eat. I'll be back."

It was one of the longest sentences he had ever spoken to me. Though a delicate flush still dusted across his cheek bones, and his eyes wavered from mine, I felt as if we had reached a turning point. I didn't want to be someone Tam feared, whether that fear was irrational or not. To be a friend, you had to rely on one another with an innate loyalty formed from trust and compassion. I hoped I could have that type of relationship with the guys. I wanted this friendship to work, more than I was willing to admit.

"You know," Elena said softly, "I'm not trying to be a bitch."

I snorted. "Could've fooled me."

From the angle she positioned herself, she effectively blocked Declan from the conversation. I knew he would be furious that Elena was purposefully excluding him, but there was nothing I could do. It hurt like a bitch to move.

"I loved them...at least I believed I loved them. It was nice to have their collective attention, you know? To feel like I was the only girl in the world, even though there were other girls." Elena's eyes turned watery with tears.

I realized, then, that she really wasn't trying to be malicious. This was a girl driven by jealousy and her concept of love. In a sense, she had her heart broken. I didn't know her history with the guys, and I didn't know the guys as well she probably did, but I could see from her sorrowful expression that she once thought the world of them. I could also see that this feeling, this love, was one-sided.

"They made me feel beautiful, special. Protected. Hell, they even gave me cheesy nicknames, but you know what I'm talking about, don't you?"

My tongue felt like sandpaper in my mouth. I swallowed, but no noise escaped me. It had never occurred to me that the guys may have only seen me as a fuck buddy. I recalled the crude way Ronan had talked about Elena and the rest of the girls. Was that what was expected of me? Was this friendship a ploy for something else? Doubts niggled my mind. I didn't want to believe that I was nothing more than a toy to them, but Elena's words planted those pesky seeds of doubt.

They *had* been using cheesy nicknames, and they *had* made me feel protected.

From what I gathered, these were boys who didn't want to fall in love - didn't want to have anything real - out of fear that they'll be hurt. Why else would they go through women so quickly?

"I can see the wheels in your head turning," Elena said. "And I'm just warning you, from woman to woman, be careful of them. They have left dozens of broken hearts behind them, and I would hate for the next one to be yours."

I couldn't ignore the sincerity in her voice. Damnit, whether it was true or not, Elena obviously believed it to be so.

Before I could respond, Ryder slid onto his knees beside me, two thin pieces of wood in his hands. They must've fallen from the roof.

"Will these work?"

"Yes," Elena sneered haughtily, ripping them from his hands. Gone was the vulnerable girl she'd revealed to me. I wondered if I imagined that entire conversation.

THE DAY WAS LONG.

I didn't know how much time passed, but it felt like months. With no natural sunlight, it was near impossible to decipher night from day. Declan had a watch, but I much preferred to be dramatic than to ask him the time.

Elena had bandaged my arm, back, and braced my leg. I had heard her sharp intake of breath when she saw the burn marks across my skin, but she didn't say anything. After she was finished, she went to her corner, and we stayed in ours.

Tamson handed me a water bottle, which I gratefully took.

"How are you feeling?" Asher asked me softly.

"Better. I really wish this place had pain meds."

Ronan leaned forward to grin at me, teeth shockingly white in his brown face. "Don't be a wuss."

"Don't be a puss," I countered.

From the other side of Ronan, Ryder let out a loud snore. I couldn't help my giggle. I wondered how the great, "sexy" Ryder would feel if he discovered that he both snored and drooled when he slept. It was no wonder he never let girls spend the night; I would be embarrassed of that too.

Calax chuckled. "Please tell him that when he gets up. It might knock him down a peg."

"Doubtful," Asher said.

I turned to smile at him, but my expression froze when I saw Declan. He had been silent thus far, more so than usual, and I feared that he felt left out. After all, we weren't using sign language to communicate with one another.

I felt a stab of guilt at my negligence.

What type of friend does that?

I squared my shoulders resolutely. It was fine. I made a mistake, but I could be better. I had to be.

Waving my hand in front of his face to garner his attention, I began to sign, "How are you feeling?"

The sullen expression contorting his features softened when his gaze met mine.

"You don't have to worry about me feeling left out," he signed quickly. "I'm used to it."

"Doesn't it get lonely?" I signed back. Asher, beside me, seemed to realize we were having a conversation and skirted out of the way. When I smiled at him, he winked at me.

"I'm used to it," Declan said, motions brisk. From the tightening of his eyes, I knew that he was lying. Nobody could be used to loneliness.

"I'm truly sorry," I said. "I'll try to do better."

If that meant facing him continuously so he could read my lips, I would. I was determined not to screw this up.

Declan was silent for a moment. His hand tapped an irregular pattern against his dust-stained jeans.

"Tell me about your friend," he said at last.

"Friend?" In my surprise, I had spoken aloud while simultaneously signing. I decided to continue speaking that way in order for him to understand me if I were to mess up a sign.

"You said that you killed your friend. What did you mean?" he continued.

Unwanted tears sprang to my eyes.

Oh Ducky. And here was Declan, with eyes almost an exact replica of my best friend's. An immeasurable amount of loss and emptiness filled me.

"You don't have to talk about it if you don't want to," Declan hurried to add, taking note of my distraught expression.

"No, it's fine." My voice was shaky. "I didn't have a lot of friends when I was younger. For obvious reasons."

I could feel Calax turning towards me, and Ronan had a thoughtful expression on his face. I offered them a gentle smile, so they knew I was okay with them listening. Taking a steadying breath, I pressed on.

"My best friend in the entire world was named Ducky. I met him at the public school after I had gotten into a fight with my parents." I scoffed at the memory. I remembered how scare I'd been at the time. Why were mommy and daddy mad at me? What had I done wrong?

Younger Adelaide was a dumbass.

"What happened?" Tam asked softly. I kept my attention on Declan as I continued.

"We became inseparable, at least in secret. I would come to visit him every morning and every afternoon that I could. He told me about his foster family and his dreams for the future. I told him about mine." I took another deep breath. "But I never told him about my parents. At least, not about their abusive tendencies. I thought it was my burden to shoulder, you know? I didn't want him to feel like he had to save me when he was struggling to save himself."

Another breath.

"On my thirteenth birthday, I told Ducky about the dinner My parents had planned for me. He showed up at the restaurant to surprise me." A small smile bloomed on my face when I remembered his slicked back hair and black suit, two sizes too big. He had looked so handsome.

My body seemed to be an epitome of contradictions, for a tear hit my turned-up lip. I instantly sobered with my next words.

"I was afraid mom and dad would hurt him, so I sent him away. I told him he meant nothing to me and that our friendship was just a pity party." I laughed, but it held no humor. "I suppose it was. He pitied me. Why else would he be my friend? I said some awful things, but you have to understand I was terrified. I knew what my parents were capable of, and I feared they would hurt him just because I loved him. Ducky left humiliated, and I watched him go. I didn't try to stop him or call him back."

A shuttering sob left me, and a hand pulled me against a muscular chest.

Declan.

His gentleness threatened to break through ever wall I constructed around myself. I wanted nothing more than to lose myself in his embrace.

I allowed him to hold me, to comfort me, for only a second before I pulled away. I had the distinct feeling that once they heard the rest of the story, they would want nothing to do with me.

The murderer.

"I watched him through the window. He was running, as if he could escape me." Another tear slid down my nose. "But he wasn't fast enough. The car came out of nowhere. I didn't...I can't..." I was sobbing now, reaching full blown hysterics. "I killed him."

Declan reached forward yet again to gather me in his arms. I didn't understand how he could touch me. Wasn't he disgusted with me? I was disgusted with myself. I was a monster.

"It was an accident, and it wasn't your fault," Asher said. I felt him behind me, hand smoothing down my untamed hair.

"I shouldn't have sent him away," I cried. All the anguish and fear I felt came pressing down on me. I had always suspected that his death was my fault, but hearing it said aloud, I knew it was. There was no doubt in my mind.

God, I hated myself.

It should've been me.

"Don't say stuff like that," Calax ordered in a harsh whisper.

Was this why I craved death? To compensate for my past sins?

"It wasn't your fault, Kitten," Ryder insisted. I hadn't even heard him wake up.

Declan pushed me away from him, and I figured that he finally had enough of me. He finally saw me for the monster I truly was.

Instead of the horror or hate I expected, his eyes widened with an undefinable emotion. It was impossible to read.

"Ducky's not dead," Declan said. A tear trailed down his cheek soon followed by a second one.

"What?" I asked, shocked. Out of everything I expected him to say, it hadn't been that. "You don't have to try to make me feel better."

"You need to-"

"I took away his future, Declan. His chance at life. At happiness. At love. He probably would've had a girlfriend named Sasha by now and lived in a cottage only two miles away from college. He would've been studying biochemical engineering, but his girlfriend would've been bitching at him to get a degree in nursing. They would've had two cats together, which they fought over after the breakup. They end up deciding on joint custody of the cats and-"

"Stop talking!" Declan signed, interrupting my hysterical rambles. I complied, clamping my mouth shut. I met Declan's smoldering stare, unshed tears gathering in my eyes. I mentally prepared myself for him to yell at me. To tell me he hated me and to go to hell, which I more than deserved.

His eyes were clear when they met mine, an endless abyss of honey woven with a light brown. Familiar.

"*I'm* Ducky."

CHAPTER 13

I had worn a light blue skirt and a white blouse to my thirteenth birthday dinner. I was always told that blue, particularly a light blue, could heighten the golden flecks in my eyes. Of course, I scoffed at such a cliché, but it still felt nice to believe, even for a moment, that I was beautiful.

The restaurant was a drive away from the resort, in a small town that spliced through the previous display of forests. It was an odd combination - tall, thick pines surrounding an assortment of glass buildings and enormous skyscrapers. It appeared as if someone had plopped a random city in the middle of the woods.

The manager greeted us by name when we entered the exclusive dining room. A three-tiered chandelier hung low in the doorway, its bright light probably supposed to be welcoming. If anything, the intermittent flicker of the bulb made me think I was walking towards my doom.

Dinner started off par for the course (read as: awkward small-talk between my parents as they both ignored me). I sipped from my water and stirred the soup idly with my spoon. I hated this restaurant. The food, despite the price, was bland, and the atmosphere was too pretentious for my tastes. My opinions, of course, didn't matter to my parents, and the fact it was my birthday wouldn't change that.

You might think it was odd that my parents, emotionally negligent and physically abusive, would remember something as mundane as my birthday. Well, it was also my mother's birthday, which was the entire reason four our celebration. They had never remembered that it was my day of birth as well.

I always wondered if that was why mom hated me - because she had to share her special day with me. She had once told me I was the worst birthday present she had ever received, as though it were my fault she couldn't hold me in until the next day. Sometimes I wished she had been pregnant-constipated and incapable of delivering me. A twisted part of me wished I had died in her womb.

The waiter arrived with our food. A steak for D.O.D., a lobster for mommy dearest, and a salad for me. Daddy told me I needed to maintain my figure to be beautiful. At that age, I had just begun developing curves. My body was no longer lithe and lightly muscled, but in the beginning stages of womanhood.

He noticed.

And he made sure to make me feel inadequate whenever the opportunity arose.

Taking another sip of water, though it did very little to subdue the bitter taste of the ranch lathered lettuce, I turned towards the front door.

I couldn't recall what drew my eyes there. Was it something inside me, like an innate knowledge of what was to come? Or was it a plea for someone to save me?

Ducky stood in the doorway, a sliver of moonlight illuminating him like a giant spotlight.

He wore his long, dark hair braided away from his face, showcasing his high cheekbones. I noticed that he dressed in a black suit, though it looked as if it belonged to a kid twice his size.

No. No.

What was he doing here?

I felt myself begin to panic. A thousand solutions floated through my mind: pretend that I wasn't here, ask to go to the bathroom and warn him away, hope that it was just a coincidence.

Before I could collect myself, Ducky walked toward our table, a bright smile alighting his face.

"Hello. You guys must be Adelaide's parents. I'm Ducky." He extended his hand, eyes warm.

My dad and mom exchanged confused glances. At least, at the moment, they didn't appear suspicious. They had always been slow. As one, I could see understanding flicker across their faces followed by surprise. I wasn't supposed to know how to human, and this boy, this Ducky, broke that rule.

Protect.

I had to protect him.

Scrambling to come up with a reasonable explanation, I watched my dad survey Ducky with more contempt than courtesy. The too long pants, the unruly hair escaping his braid, the birthmark on his pale throat.

"Addie," my father said with a deadly calm. "You never told me that you met a friend."

I blurted the first thing I could think of. "He's not my friend."

Dad lifted a manicured eyebrow, and Ducky blanched as if I had slapped him.

"He seems to think you are friends," Daddy said evenly. He cut into his steak, eyes never leaving mine. Yes, because it's completely normal to play with knives while glaring at your daughter.

"Oh please," I said with an eye roll. "As if I would ever be friends with someone like him. Have you seen his clothes? Pathetic. And that hair? Maybe he's trying to be mistaken as a girl."

I knew I hit his sore spot when Ducky's face paled, and his lower lip trembled.

Ducky, I'm sorry. Please forgive me.

Protect him.

"No, I'm not his friend. He was just a boy I took pity on. I was nice to him once, and suddenly he thinks we're friends." I laughed. Did my parents not realize how fake that laugh was?

Turning towards Ducky, I sneered as if I found him repulsive. If anything, I found myself repulsive. At that moment, I hated myself.

Protect him.

"You can leave now. God, the creepy stalker look doesn't look good on you."

Dad clamped his lips together as if to hold in a laugh. Mother, however, had already turned back towards her lobster.

I watched Ducky's face fall, surprise giving way to betrayal. He looked at me as if I had ripped his spine from his body, spat on it, and then fed it to my dog.

For as long as I lived, I would never be able to forget that anguished expression.

And then he was running. In his haste to escape, he stumbled into a passing waiter.

And I laughed.

I fucking *laughed*.

I watched him as he ran through the doorway, into the road. He glanced back, tears on his cheeks, and I resisted the urge to run to him.

I'm so sorry.

These were words I couldn't say. Looking back, I sometimes wished that I accidently spoke my thoughts aloud back
then. That particular trait wouldn't pop up until a couple
months later.

Ducky's face was still turned towards mine, so he didn't
see the truck barreling down the street. He didn't see the
driver attempt to slam on his brakes in a desperate attempt
to avoid the small boy in the road. He did see my face, my
mouth opened in a scream he couldn't hear. His brow drew
down, head tilting to the side.

And then the truck plowed into him.

I screamed until my throat was hoarse, and I haven't
stopped since.

I REPLAYED DECLAN'S WORDS, sure I had heard him wrong. He
probably meant to say that he knew Ducky. Maybe he actually said, "I'm Lucky." That was a more plausible explanation
than the one he gave me.

Ducky was dead. I had seen him die. My parents told me
as much.

This man, this Declan, was not my Ducky.

"I don't know what type of fucking game you're trying to
play, but I'm..." A sob broke through my chest. I knew Declan
was icy, but I had never suspected him capable of such
cruelty. This was unforgivable.

Without taking his eyes from mine, Declan pulled down
the collar of his shirt. Staining his tanned skin was a dark
birthmark.

Ducky's birthmark.

No. No.

I hadn't even realized I was speaking aloud until Declan grabbed my hand in both of his. I shook my head, as if that action could somehow change what I saw.

"Your name is Declan, not Ducky," I insisted. I could barely breathe. My heart, my damn heart, thumped in my chest like a sledgehammer. It dared to hope while my brain warned me against it.

"My nickname is Ducky," Declan signed. He, too, had tears in his eyes. At some point, the other guys must've left us alone. I no longer felt the heat from their bodies.

"No. This can't...you can't...this can't be happening."

I began to sob in earnest now, overwhelmed from the influx of information he tried to relay. He couldn't be Ducky, I knew that, but I couldn't ignore the facts slapping me in the face. No, they weren't just slapping me. They were full-on bitch punching me while a train ran over me.

On closer inspection, Declan had the same bone structure as Ducky. High cheekbones, chiseled jawline, tapered waist. While Ducky was lithe, Declan was muscled. While Ducky had long hair, Declan had short, at least on the sides. While Ducky was pale, Declan was tanned by consistent sunlight exposure.

While Ducky could hear, Declan was deaf.

But...

But the birthmark. The crescent shaped brown patch marring his skin. Ducky, too, had that on his neck, almost caressing his collarbone.

Something made me lean forward to brush my fingers against Declan's skin. I didn't know what I was hoping for. For it to be makeup? For it not to be?

The birthmark was real, and the fact sent an undefinable tingle through my body.

Voice quiet, as if I was afraid anything louder would force him to laugh in my face, I murmured, "Ducky?"

"Addie."

And then he wrapped his arms around me, extra mindful of my injuries. I pressed my face into his neck, crying, relishing in the comfort and heat he emitted.

This was Ducky. My Ducky. My best friend, and the only person I had ever truly loved.

I pulled away from him, eyes bloodshot, to see he wasn't faring much better. His own eyes were glassy with unshed tears. With a trembling hand, he pushed a strand of knotted hair behind my ear.

I didn't care that I was in pain. I didn't care that I had a broken leg, a scarred back, or an arm that was losing feeling by the second.

All I cared about was the handsome boy in front of me.

"You're alive," I whispered, pulling back to face him. His eyes remained focused intently on my lips as he read my words.

"Yes."

"Why didn't you...why didn't you tell me?" I sobbed, my relief transforming into anger. I had spent years - years! - believing I had killed my best friend. I knew he had been pissed at me, I wouldn't have blamed him, but this? Ignoring me after I witnessed him get hit by a truck? Making me believe him dead? That was borderline torture.

"I tried!" Declan - Ducky - insisted. His eyes grew wide. "Your parents said you didn't want to talk to me. They said you..." His hands faltered as if he was unsure what else he wanted to say.

"They said what?" I asked calmly. Too calmly.

"They said you never once asked about me. They said you laughed when the truck came."

I exploded. "And you believed them? After everything we'd been through?"

I knew I was yelling, and I knew the effort was futile, but

I couldn't help it (and yes, I understood the irony of yelling at a deaf guy). Ducky and I had spent years together. He was my best friend and I, his. How could he just believe I would throw that away? That I faked it for all those years?

"What was I supposed to think? After what you said to me?"

"I did that to protect you!" I screeched. Calax, on the opposite side of the room, looked as if he wanted to run towards me, but Asher held him back.

"I didn't know that." Declan's movements turned jerky, his agitation reflected in his sign language.

I didn't know what to do. One part of me wanted to burrow myself inside of Declan, to relish in the familiarity of my best friend, while another part of me wanted to run in the opposite direction.

Despite my outburst, I knew my anger wasn't directed at him but at myself.

It occurred to me suddenly that Declan hadn't escaped the accident unscathed. He lost something when the truck came barreling toward him, more than just a pathetic friend. He lost his hearing.

It was all my fault.

I had felt guilty before, every day since Ducky's accident, but this was a different type. This was something physical, something I could reach out and touch. Seeing Declan now, his attention riveted on my lips as he read my words, I wanted to cry.

Scream.

Hurt.

I wanted to hurt myself, and I hated that thought. I didn't like it when my mind went to such a dark, depressing place.

"Addie," Ducky signed, but then moved his hands to his lap. He didn't know what to say, but that was good. I wouldn't know how to respond.

"I think I need to be alone for a moment."

"Addie, please, I need for you to know..."

"Please, Ducky. I just need to be alone." I met his eyes, so familiar and sincere, before placing my head in my hands. I wanted to wallow in my self-pity and self-hatred. I was so fucked up, I knew that. I just...I just needed someone, and I had no one.

Declan was silent for only a moment before he nodded slowly. As he scrambled to his feet, I watched, almost mesmerized, as he wiped soot and debris from his clothing.

It hurt to look at him.

God, did it hurt.

As Declan left, Calax came over. Without a word, he sat down beside me.

"I don't want to talk," I whispered.

He grunted. "I know."

And we sat.

WE SAT for over an hour in companionable silence. Anytime someone came near us, Calax would glare at them until they scurried away. I had never been more appreciative of his asshole-ish-ness than I was at that moment.

Only Tamson dared to venture closer to me, and that was to only give me a can of beans he'd found and a bottle of water. I eyed the items with distaste.

I didn't deserve to eat. I deserved to waste away like the scum I was.

"Baby," Calax murmured, "I hate it when you think that way."

"I'm a horrible person," I said, squeezing my eyes shut in a desperate attempt to will the tears away. "How can you even look at me? I disgust myself."

"Don't say that." His hand clamped down on my good knee. "You're strong and brave and a fighter. I am so lucky I have gotten to know you."

"How can you say that? Declan's your friend, and it's because of me that he's deaf." Saying the words aloud made them all too real.

"Did you know, that whenever Declan would talk about the incident that took his hearing, he never mentioned it as the worst thing that happened to him?" Calax asked. I bit my lip but didn't reply. No, I didn't know that.

And I doubted that to be true. He had lost his hearing - his ability to motherfucking hear - and Calax dared to say that wasn't the worst thing that had happened to him?

"When he talks about that day, he refers to it as the day he lost his best friend." Though his voice was gruff, I didn't think Calax was capable of anything else, he kept it gentle. His hand squeezed my knee in reassurance. "Of course, I didn't know he was talking about you, and I didn't know this mysterious friend was even still alive, but it was you that he talked about. He really..." He coughed, as if the words had gotten stuck in his throat. "He really loved you. Loves you."

I snorted. "He hates me."

Declan's hostility at our first meeting made perfect sense now. I'm surprised that he hadn't straight up stabbed me. I would've.

"He never hated you. He was heartbroken." Calax removed his hand from my knee, and I immediately missed its warmth. His hand grabbed mine.

"That was actually one of the reasons why he broke up with his last girlfriend. Because of you."

"Because of me?"

"Because he wouldn't stop talking about you. He loved you."

I wiped at my eyes, the gesture proving ineffective when more tears escaped.

"Why are you telling me all of this?"

Calax grew silent. If his hand hadn't tightened over mine, I would've assumed he hadn't heard me. His jaw clenched.

"Because I want you to be happy, Addie. You deserve all the love and happiness in the world."

"Including yours?" I didn't know what possessed me to say that. But staring up at his handsome face, shadowed jawline and keen eyes, I found that I couldn't regret it. There had been something brewing between Calax and me for a while now. I had never dared look at it too closely, but, just then, I wasn't thinking clearly. I was consumed by an unbearable pain and the overpowering need to be loved and love someone back.

Calax's face softened. The change was drastic on him, as if he suddenly became an entirely different person. His large hand cupped my cheek.

Was he going to kiss me?

Did I want him to?

Someone began to scream, and I wrenched my gaze in the direction it came from. I recognized the girl running into the room, eyes wide and fearful.

Shannon.

"Are you okay?" Asher asked, hurrying to meet her at the entrance. She let out a strangled sob.

"It's...it's   Dave!   There's...He's   not...something's happening to him. He's not acting like himself. He's..." Shannon leaned forward and vomited.

Black blood.

When she looked back up, her eyes no longer were the emerald green I remembered. As I watched, horrified, red began to eat away the original color as if her pupil was bleeding. Something black crawled beneath her pale skin.

"Shannon?" This came from Ryder as he hesitantly stepped up behind Asher. Shannon cocked her head to the side as she considered him.

"Now you pay attention to me?" she asked in a hoarse voice. Before Ryder could respond, Shannon pounced on him.

CHAPTER 14

Things I never thought I would see in my life:

    1. My dad smiling at me

2. Calax smiling at me

3. A crazy hostess lunging at my new friend with feral eyes.

Apparently, I was rocking a solid two out of three.

Like a switch was flipped, my mind turned off. I couldn't - wouldn't - watch Shannon hurt Ryder. Too much pain and suffering already punctuated my life.

I squeezed my eyes shut as if that small gesture could keep me hidden from the world.

Why was the world such a desolate place? When did it start going to hell?

I slapped my hands over my ears to muffle the sounds. Despite this barrier, I still heard the enraged snarl.

Shannon.

I didn't know how, but I knew that sound came from her.

What the hell was happening?

The only two solutions I could consider were a virus or a

drug, both of which seemed scary beyond belief. The latter, though, raised more questions than answers. What type of drug would both Shannon and Buttlicker be taking?

Come to think of it, what did they have in common in the first place? If it was virus, which I had begun to believe it was, they must've come into contact at one point, right?

And how was this virus transmitted? Air? Saliva?

My head began to pound with the mounting number of questions.

I risked opening one eyelid, only one, before wishing I hadn't. I couldn't look away,

Shannon was looming over top of Ryder. Somehow, her small, dainty body easily incapacitated his much larger, more muscular one. Where did she get all that strength from?

I froze in shock, growing numb as I watched Ryder attempt to push her off him. Seeming indifferent to his efforts, she bared her teeth in an aggressive display. Asher grabbed at Shannon, but she flicked him away as if he was nothing more than a pesky bug. He came back, muscles flexing and chest heaving from exertion, and grabbed underneath her armpits. It was obvious that both boys were trying their best not to hurt her.

"Shannon!" Another girl cried. She was slightly older than me, mid-twenties I would guess, and wore the pink pleated skirt that identified her as a waitress at Rosie's Diner. "What the hell are you doing?"

Shannon's head whipped towards the intruding voice, lips pulling back into a malicious smirk.

"Hannah," Shannon said stiffly, and then, with her attention diverted to the other girl, she attacked. Her teeth dug into Hannah's neck. All I could do was watch, unable to move and unable to help. Blood splattered the wall, Shannon's face, and the boy beside Hannah. I could see the white of the bones in the older girl's pale neck

Somebody began to scream, but that sound only seemed to spur Shannon on.

She turned towards the boy next to Hannah and began clawing at his face. Blood cascaded down his cheeks like tear drops; deep gashes marred his freckled skin.

And Shannon...

Her face morphed something I would never be able to forget. Gone was the flirtatious girl who occasionally said hi to me in passing. Her blond hair, once a vibrant sheen, now had balding spots. Her porcelain skin rippled like a reflective pool of water, veins darkening and twitching beneath the surface. She barely seemed to process that her fingernails were getting pulled off with each desperate swipe at the now dead body. Blood pooled around them all, staining Shannon's uniform and skin. If you hadn't seen her attack, if you hadn't heard their screams, you might've believed that all three of them were lovers in an intimate embrace.

Transfixed on the macabre sight in front me, I barely registered another figure entering the dimly lit room. He, too, had flesh dangling precariously from his face, as if he had pulled at the skin repeatedly. His hands twitched, curled into claws by his sides, and his blood red eyes surveyed the room with a predatory-like awareness.

And then they landed on me.

Prime prey, all broken and pathetic against the wall. In truth, if I were a carnivore, I would've eaten myself a long time ago. If, of course, I could eat myself. Not that it was possible to do so without dying. But if I could live and eat myself...

Good god. I really was insane.

The new guy took a threatening step in my direction, and I attempted to press myself further into the wall.

Nothing to see here. Just wall plaster. I'm just wall plaster.

I squeezed my eyes shut. If I was going to die, I really

didn't want to see it coming. Why couldn't my death be peaceful? Was that too much to ask? It occurred to me that I deserved this horrific death. Monsters like me got what they deserved in the end it seemed.

I heard the rustling of fabric, but no pain came to me. I dared to open my eyes, startled to see Tam planted in front of me, hands raised in a defensive stance.

The two men went at each other, a flurry of fists and snarls (the latter of which came from Mr. Zombie). I didn't dare even breathe, afraid that any movement or sound would distract Tam.

A rough hand grabbed my arm, and I jerked away.

"No time, Princess," a familiar voice said in a breathless whisper. Ronan.

Before I could gasp, he threw me over his shoulder in a fireman carry. My body, aching everywhere, hung like dead weight. Slightly irrational, I couldn't help but pity Ronan for having to carry my heavy ass. It wasn't that I was fat, necessarily, but the bandages and makeshift cast on my leg definitely weighed me down.

Not the time, Addie, I mentally berated myself.

Shannon had turned away from her victims, teeth bared as she faced the newcomer. Tamson lay splayed face down on the ground.

I felt a moment of panic before I saw him twitch, and Declan helped him to his feet.

Ronan began to run down the hallway, but with the way he held me, I was still able to see the scene we were leaving behind. I watched Shannon attack the new zombie (because what else could he be?). They clawed and bit at each other, blood coating their skin.

An older woman, who sat on the far side of the room, got up and attempted to walk around them. They paused mid-fight, and in unison, they turned towards the woman, grabbing and beginning to eat her. Actually eat her.

It was something that I didn't think could happen in real life, only in movies. Their teeth broke through skin.

Stop.

Please stop.

Try as I might, I couldn't get the words to leave my mouth. Large spikes of terror shot through me, drowning out any surprise I might've felt at their actions.

I tried to process everything I had just seen. I tried to put an emotion on the feelings churning in my stomach or the haziness clouding my thoughts. I needed to think coherently; I needed to understand what just happened.

Nothing made sense anymore.

Ronan led me into a new, unfamiliar room and carefully lowered me into a chair. I winced at the pain firing through my leg but attempted to tamp down on my urge to cry. There were more important things to focus on than my stupid injury.

The rest of the guys, and a couple of other people that had been in the other room with us, including Elena and Bikini, ran in behind us. Calax and Declan slammed and held the door shut while Ryder, with the help of Asher, pushed a fridge in front of it. The boys continued adding items to create an makeshift barricade that, hopefully, would keep out the rest of the world.

I didn't have high hopes.

I'd seen plenty of horror movies. Wasn't this where we all died? Trapped, confined in a small space, lacking resources, and the only light reliant on a faulty-at-best generator. I mean, at least I wasn't the bitchy girl. They always died first in those movies.

"Actually," Ryder said casually, sitting down beside me. "It's the black guy."

"I'll write you a eulogy," I deadpanned. Ryder tried to smile, but it was clear he had to force it.

With the most pressing, immediate threat neutralized for now, I took the opportunity to look around the room we hunkered down in.

There was a long table in the center, surrounded by miscellaneous chairs that didn't seem to have a set style: a lawn chair, a plastic one, and even a recliner. The room was relatively barren besides a microwave on the far counter and a fridge. A time-clock was on the opposite wall. There was an adjacent staircase, but with the amount of clutter, I didn't expect us to get out of there anytime soon.

It was the fridge the guys went to first, still pressed against the door. Empty, mostly, besides for a water bottle and a juice box. Declan grabbed them both.

"What the fuck are we going to do?" Elena screamed. She was huddled together with the group of girls from earlier. She no longer was the calm and composed girl fawning over the boys. She looked absolutely terrified just then, her face streaked with tears and hair matted with dry blood.

"I don't know," Asher said, not unkindly. His answer, however, didn't placate Elena. She stormed over to him, tiny hands curled into tinier fists. Before I could react, she pounded said fists against Asher's chest.

"Cut that shit out!" I snapped, an almost incandescent fury burning through me at seeing Elena hurt Asher. Or, at least, attempting to hurt. I was almost positive Asher's chest was made of steel. "If we want out of this alive, we have to work together and that means no petty fights amongst ourselves."

I glanced at each individual face as I spoke to emphasize my point.

Besides the guys, Elena, and Bikini, I didn't recognize

anyone else in the room with us. There was a cluster of girls that I assumed were with Elena, and a young man wearing a white, lifeguard shirt. An older couple held onto each other in the far corner, away from everybody else, and another man stood stoutly besides Declan, eyes scanning the room intensely. I felt momentarily relieved that there were no children with us.

I wouldn't be able to handle that pressure.

"Okay," I said, once I'd gathered everyone's attention. "Here's what we know. Shannon and another guy-"

"Dave," the man supplied. I nodded gratefully.

"Yes, Shannon and Dave are not themselves."

"They're fucking zombies!" Bikini cried.

"We don't know that," Tam said. "It could be a new drug in circulation or a simple virus that, somehow, is messing with their brain."

"We have to kill them," the man said, crossing his arms over his chest. From the black leather he wore, I guessed he was a part of the resort's security.

"We can't kill them, Brad!" Asher sounded aghast at the prospect.

"Those...*things* aren't Shannon and Dave anymore. For all we know, Hannah and Liam could be like them now. We don't know what the hell we're dealing with," the man, Brad apparently, insisted.

"There must be another way."

"How long do you think it will be until someone comes for us?" I asked no one in particular.

"Knowing Sarge, there's already a group digging us out," Elena huffed. I blinked at the name.

The mysterious Sarge. Who was he, and how would he be able to gather the manpower to save us?

Instead of asking all that, I nodded seriously.

"Maybe we should just wait it out."

Brad's hands clenched by his sides.

"For how long? We have no food in here and only one fucking water bottle! It might take them days to get us out, if not weeks! I vote we kill those bastards outside and grab our water supply!"

"Those bastards," snapped Asher, his voice sharper than I had ever heard before, "are our friends. You heard them speak. Some cognitive function remained in their minds. I believe that they can be saved."

Brad stepped forward until he was nose-to-nose with Asher.

"We're saving murderers now, boy?" he asked. He pointed an accusatory finger in Asher's face, but Asher swatted it away.

"Don't fucking act like you're so much better than me. What you're suggesting is murder. Would you kill someone if they were high on weed and acting crazy?"

"This is different, and you know it!"

"Enough!" My voice broke through their fight like the crack of a whip. Both men turned towards me, eyes flashing. "You two fighting isn't going to help anything."

Brad's expression turned almost thoughtful as he considered me.

"Why don't we use the bitch as bait? Allow the Ragers to munch on her while we grab the water and food we collected."

His proclamation was met with a chorus of threats. The boys immediately stood in front of me, a protective wall of muscle.

I couldn't help but think back to what he said. Rager? I supposed that description was fitting towards what we saw. Shannon and Dave had appeared to be almost in a rage, as if their entire mindset was focused on the primal hunt and the hunt alone.

"Don't fucking look at her!" Ryder snapped, jarring me from my thoughts. The boys were still facing off with Brad. They all seemed to be trembling with barely suppressed anger.

"She's injured. Probably bleeding out if her arm is any indication. Why wouldn't we sacrifice her for the good of us all?"

"Do you fucking hear yourself?" Tam exploded. My sweet, shy Tam. I didn't like it when he was angry. Everything inside of me wanted to walk over to him and touch him. Soothe him.

"Which one would it be? Those monsters' lives or that girl's? You can't have both."

"You even try to touch her, and you'll fucking die," Calax threatened.

I appreciated him standing up for me, but...

"Maybe he's right."

Every head turned my way. Grimacing under their combined stares, I focused on the brace supporting my leg.

"We don't know how long we're going to be down here. What if it takes weeks for them to find us? I mean, does anyone know that we're here? Most people would go to the level just above us because only a select few had keys to this one. Brad's right that we need the water and food we collected."

"No fucking way," Calax hissed.

"Don't even think about it, Princess."

Declan just glared.

"I'm injured; that much is obvious. I'll be lucky if I'm even able to keep this damn leg." Tears filled my eyes, but I refused, absolutely refused, to let them spill. I met each boy's stare before turning towards Declan. Towards Ducky. His face was impassive.

"I have done so many horrible things, some of which can never be forgiven. But I can do this. I can save lives. Maybe, just maybe, this will redeem myself enough where I can die without hating myself."

For a moment, Declan continued to stare at me, face apathetic. The first crack I saw in his front was the trembling of his lips. His eyes began blinking rapidly in an attempt to hold his tears at bay. I watched with rapt attention as he fell to his knees in front of me.

And then he spoke. His voice was hoarse, from years without use, but it was still a voice I loved dearly. It was Ducky's voice.

"No."

One word.

Like a domino falling over, the boys took that as indication to move. They surrounded me protectively, eyes throwing daggers at the other occupants in this room.

"No way in hell."

"Not happening, Kitten. You're stuck with us."

"We protect our own."

Brad sputtered. "It's her fucking choice whether or not she wants to." To me, he said, "Don't be selfish. You have to think about the others."

"Why don't you be the bait, then?" Ronan asked. His muscles coiled tight under his shirt, like a snake preparing to attack. I put my hand on his bicep to calm him, and he deflated marginally.

"I'm not injured," he huffed.

Calax took a menacing step forward. "We could change that."

"Enough, okay?" I snapped. I tugged at Calax's arm until he turned to face me. His wild eyes bounced all around me before finally resting on my face. They seemed to have trouble focusing. "Enough."

"She's right." This voice came from an unlikely ally. Elena stepped closer to Brad, head tilted domineeringly. "For now, we are fine. We'll see how long it takes the cavalry to come. Who knows? The situation might look different tomorrow."

CHAPTER 15

*T*he fever set in that night.

I tossed and turned, but it did little to smother the flames attacking my skin. Sweat beaded my forehead, dripping down my cheeks and seeping into my clothes. At some point, the power must've gone out. We used our phone lights for as long as we could before they, too, went dead.

It was dark, almost unnaturally so, like a spilt cauldron of ink. I couldn't even see my hands in front of my face let alone the other occupants of the room.

"How are you feeling?" Tam whispered. He brushed his hand against my forehead. We previously had taken ice from the freezer in order to lower my fever, but our supply had long since dwindled.

My teeth clattered as I spoke, "Shitty."

"Calvary is going to be here soon, Princess," Ryder said from the other side of me.

Even I knew that was bull crap.

My body alternated between fits of intense heat and a numb coldness. I tried to escape these episodes with drastic movements, but that only brought pain to my leg and arm.

From experience, I knew not to whimper. Whenever I outwardly expressed my pain, the boys would react with cries of their own. I wanted to spare them of this as much as I could.

Though I couldn't communicate with Declan at all, I felt his presence behind me. He currently had my head in his lap, gently stroking my hair away from my sweaty face. Calax had grown frantic, pulling at the barricade in front of the staircase ever since my fever set in. I could hear him then, mumbling under his breath, and cussing at anyone who came too close to him. He was desperate for an escape, desperate to save me, but I knew the effort was futile.

"Tell me something about you," I said softly, squeezing Tam's hand. I wasn't sure if he would be willing to share, what with his shyness, but the silence was almost oppressive. Even Elena had stopped her bitching when my condition worsened. They all thought I was going to die.

But I had dealt with worse, and I would be damned before something as insignificant as an infection and broken leg took me in.

"Well," Tam began hesitantly. I heard his teeth clench together, and I gave his hand another squeeze.

"You don't have to tell me anything if you're not comfortable."

"It's fine." He lowered his voice to a whisper. This was just between him and me; everybody else faded into the background. "I didn't have the best childhood either. My birth parents abused drugs, and I was adopted by my grandma when I was five." He paused for a second, and, when he spoke next, I could hear the smile in his voice. "She was the best damn mother I could've ever had. She made sure I wanted for nothing. I was...a shy kid, to put it mildly, but she never made me feel bad for being exactly who I was. She supported me and my decision to join MMA." I squeezed our connected hands when he paused again. From his shuddering breath, I knew that the next part of the story wouldn't have a happily ever after. "She died when I was twelve."

I wanted to tell him that I was sorry, but I knew he didn't want my pity. There was a distinct difference between sympathy and empathy; you never really understand something until you'd been through it yourself. The only death I had experienced had been Ducky's, and apparently, that hadn't even been a real death.

"I moved into a foster home shortly after. They were nice and all, but I couldn't live there. They always stared at me with pity, with 'poor-parentless-kid' looks. So I ran away.

"I was alone on the streets until I was thirteen when I came across two boys playing baseball at the local park. I asked them if I could play, but the dickhead said no."

"In my defense," Ryder said with a hint of a smile in his voice, "you looked fucking creepy."

"I was homeless, you ass," Tam laughed, but then instantly sobered. "Yeah, the dick was Ryder and the other kid was Sarge. I got to talking with them, and they told me about their school. Sarge helped me apply, and the rest is history."

"So you got your happy ending," I said airily. He leaned forward to kiss the top of my head.

"Maybe."

We were silent, each lost in our own thoughts. Declan's fingers against my cheeks were the only constant.

Somewhere in the darkness, Calax let out a string of curses, and Asher muttered something in response. Probably trying to calm him. Someone on the opposite side of the room was rearranging furniture. Why someone would do that when it was pitch black was beyond my comprehension.

I was suddenly very tired, overwhelmingly so. My eyelids fluttered as I struggled to keep them opened.

"You can't go to sleep yet, Kitten," Ryder said. "You have to stay awake."

"I'm tired," I mumbled, my words an inarticulate mesh.

"I know, but you have to stay awake."

The boys began talking about random things. Funny stories from school, Ryder's crazy ex-girlfriend (though Ryder insisted that they had never really dated), and plans for when we escaped. Every once in a while, I felt Declan's fingers feather against my pulse as if to make sure I was still alive. After the tenth time, I felt slightly offended that he doubted my ability to survive.

"Nobody's doubting you honey," Tam said. "We're just worried."

"Don't be. I'll be fine." My voice came out hoarse, scratchy almost, contradicting my statement.

"Did you know what I wanted to be when I was younger?" Ryder asked me suddenly. I blinked at the abrupt change of topic.

"A musician that is a horrible flirt?" I offered, and I heard him chuckle.

"I actually wanted to be a realtor."

"A realtor?" I asked in disbelief. Most kids said something along the lines of "doctor" or "astronaut". I had to admit that Ryder was one of a kind.

"My foster dad was one, and I wanted to be just like him when I grew up."

"And then you fell in love with music?" I guessed.

He agreed. "And then I fell in love with music."

"Do you sing?"

His hand lightly trailed across my collarbone leaving goosebumps in its wake.

"I do."

"Could you sing me something?"

If I was going to die, I at least wanted to die listening to this man's beautiful, raspy voice.

"You're not going to die, but I do agree that my voice is beautiful."

And then he began to sing. It was soulful, magical, as if he was transporting me to another place and time. I felt each word like a knife in my heart. He sung of love lost and hope for the future.

I could've listened to him all day. I might've, if I hadn't felt myself start to doze off. I tried my hardest to resist the pulls of sleep, but my body was weak and weighed down.

And it was so tempting...

I only had a second to think that sleep might be a really bad idea before darkness consumed my thoughts.

I DREAMT I was thirteen again, watching the truck barreling down on Ducky. I watched his body flip, like a gymnast doing a complicated routine, before his corpse settled on the ground, a puddle of blood surrounding him.

Unlike my past self, I ran towards where Ducky was sprawled. Dropping to my knees beside him, I sobbed into his hair.

His eyes snapped open suddenly. His face gradually began to shift, skin tightening over his bones to rid himself of his baby fat. Dark brown hair, currently grazing his waist, shrunk back into his head until it resembled the hair I was now familiar with.

Declan.

"Why did you do this to me?" he asked, voice devoid of any emotion. There was no lisp to his words, no stuttering.

This is what Declan would've sounded like if he hadn't lost his hearing.

THE DARKNESS WE CRAVE

"I'm sorry, Ducky. I am so sorry."

"You deserve to die." His hand grabbed my wrist, and I let out a squeal as his fingers tightened. They were going to leave a nasty bruise.

"Declan, you're hurting me. Please."

"And you didn't hurt me? You deserve this. You deserve everything that's happening to you."

"I'm sorry."

His eyes narrowed on me.

"You're only sorry because you got caught."

I woke up to someone's hand over my mouth.

At first, I thought it was one of the boys, unintentionally being aggressive. But then the person leaned down until his mouth was by my ear.

"Don't say a word, or I'll cut the throat of your deaf friend."

Brad.

My muscles tensed up, but I managed a weak nod.

To be honest, that wasn't the first time I had been awoken by a strange man. However, it was the first time that I could remember being more pissed than scared. Couldn't he have just let me sleep?

To my right, I heard the familiar roar of Ryder's snore. On the opposite side, Tam's breathing was nice and even. I didn't know where Declan was, but I thought I heard Ronan mumble something in his sleep near my head.

Before I could smack the dickhead that dared disturb my sleep, he lifted me into his arms. Whatever protest I might've conjured died on my lips when I felt the press of a knife to my neck.

Well damn. He was taking this kidnapping thing pretty seriously.

He walked with startling accuracy through the snoring crowd, only stopping once we reached whatever destination he had in mind. How he could see in the dark was beyond me, and I didn't dare ask. I mean, I wasn't in the mood to be knifed just yet.

I let out a whimper as he hoisted me to one arm, like I was a toddler getting carried around by her parents.

"Quiet," he hissed. Well excuse me if my cry of pain wasn't silent enough for you.

Bastard.

I heard what sounded like a door opening, and then we were walking again. It suddenly occurred to me where we were going. This theory was only reinforced when he switched on his phone light, and I saw the familiar hall outside of the break room.

He was sacrificing me to Shannon and what's-his-name.

And he had light while we had been struggling in the darkness.

I honestly couldn't tell you which one pissed me off more. I fucking hated the darkness, probably even more than I hated getting sacrificed to zombies.

Deeming me capable of walking, he dropped me unceremoniously onto the ground. I let out a cry as my leg jammed into the wooden floor. The pain was immediate and undescribable. No words could articulate the flames of fire creeping up my legs, my nerves, burning me alive.

Damn him. Damn him to the deepest pit of hell.

"Keep swearing all you want, Sunshine. I'm doing us all a favor."

"Which is what exactly?" I grunted. My legs wobbled underneath me as I attempted to haul myself to my feet. The bastard had dropped me too far away from a wall to be able to use it to steady myself. Instead, I was forced to awkwardly crawl onto my good knee, unsavory substances and grit clinging to my hands. This position caused my weak, bloody arm to scream in protest, but I ignored it.

"Are you just going to leave me here?" I whispered harshly. Brad - Damn Brad - had stealthily moved to a branching hallway, the light from his phone sufficing his features in a yellow glow. The bastard had the nerve to smile at me.

"I'm going to wait until they're distracted, and then grab the supplies. Are you really so selfish that you can't see the good your sacrifice will bring?"

I rolled my eyes because, really, what more could I do?

"Are you really so stupid that you can't see the death that will come to you when the guys realize what you did?"

"They'll thank me in the long run. Once we survive." He paused. "I'm sorry that it had to be this way."

From the sincerity in his voice, I realized he was telling the truth. He was sorry, but, in his mind, there was no other alternative. It was me or them, and he had obviously made his choice.

I couldn't say I blamed him. From his perspective, I was nothing more than some rich, bitchy girl. I had everything while he had nothing. It was the same story, the same cliché, and there was nothing I could do to change his mentality. He was the hero in his story and I, the villain.

It never really struck me how easily death could occur. It was just a word. How many times had I wished death would claim me? How many times had I wished that I would survive?

I supposed that I had an unhealthy relationship with good old death. It was my constant companion. I had gotten close to meeting him too many times to count.

I could admit that I was scared when the light was

snatched away, leaving nothing but the familiar darkness. My heart thumped erratically in my chest, threatening to break free from my ribcage.

Somewhere in the darkness, I heard a growl.

Well shit.

The growl was immediately followed by a voice.

"Come out, come out wherever you are."

Okay, let me just give you all a word of advice. If a creepy zombie-like creature asks you to come out, you stay fucking put. Or you curl up in a ball and cry - any of those are acceptable responses.

I didn't dare to breathe. Hell, I didn't even dare think, afraid that my idiotic mind would speak the thought aloud. It always happened when I was panicking.

And I was most definitely panicking.

Stay calm, Addie. Stay calm.

I wondered if I would feel pain when I died. I wondered if I would scream in agony or if death would be a merciful escape. I hoped for the latter but not for the most obvious reasons.

I was afraid that if I screamed, the boys would come running. If I was going to be sacrificed, those boys were going to reap the benefits.

They were my first friends, and they would be my last.

Depressing, even by my standards.

Something moved ahead of me. It sounded like finger-nails dragging against the wall.

Okay, so that was slightly terrifying.

I squeezed my eyes shut and waited. That was all I could do. Wait for death.

Exactly how I wanted to spend my Friday night.

My eyes were still closed when Shannon jumped on me. They remained closed as her teeth gnawed on my neck, ripping apart skin and tendons. They remained closed when somebody began to shout, and then gunshots fired.

I barely processed Shannon's dead body overtop of mine.

People rushed to and fro. I heard a voice that sounded like Calax's, but it was weak at best. Two men hoisted me onto a stretcher, and I was carted up what seemed like a staircase.

A staircase?

Did help finally come?

I dared to open my eyes then.

The moon was the first thing I saw, followed by the red and blue flashing lights of numerous fire trucks and ambulances. It was the ambulance that I was led into, my weak body and even weaker mind trying to hold onto consciousness.

A woman touched my neck.

My leg.

My arm.

Voices.

So many voices.

Tired.

And then I slept.

CHAPTER 16

The first time I almost died, I had been nine.

Surprisingly, the blow hadn't been delivered by Daddy or Mommy, but by a business associate of my father. His name had been Luka, but I would forever refer to him as Evil Bastard.

To EB, I was nothing more than a pawn to use against D.O.D.. I had tried to tell him that I meant nothing to the old fart, that the love he gave me was conditional at best. If, that is, you could even call it love.

That didn't matter to EB.

I remembered his hand, steady on the gun, as he lowered it towards my stomach. I remembered how I begged for my life, begged for this man to understand that I was innocent in this battle between families.

A battle that I had yet to fully understand.

That didn't stop the man from pulling the trigger.

For a moment, I had been stunned, unable to fully comprehend what had just happened. Had he really shot me?

My body lurched forward, and my hands instinctively

went to my stomach. The fabric of my shirt was stained with blood.

There was so much blood.

MY EYELIDS FLUTTERED OPEN, but immediately slammed closed again when a bright light blinded me.

Throbbing. My head was throbbing, as if someone was stabbing my brain repeatedly with a rusty knife.

I dared to open my eyes again.

The first thing I saw was the bright, pink cast on my leg. Turning my head, I noted the white bandages on my arm.

What the hell?

Taking in the rest of the room, I realized that I was lying on a small cot, with only a thin blanket wrapped around my waist. I must've moved at some point during my sleep. The pungent stench of bleach assaulted my nose. I always hated that particular smell; it reminded me of the frequent beatings I had been forced to endure and the numerous resulting hospital trips.

A hospital.

But not the resort's hospital. No, I didn't recognize this room with its opened blinds and assortment of medical tools.

For a moment, I remained motionless, listening to the steady patter of my heartbeat.

I tried to recall how I ended up in this sparsely lit room with its white walls and gray bedding.

Brad had tried to kill me, hadn't he? Yes, I remembered that vividly. The bastard had wanted to feed me to Shannon! Fury churned in my stomach.

And then what happened?

I vaguely remembered gunshots, and then nothing. What had happened? How had I ended up here?

"I see that you're awake," a kind voice said. This voice belonged to a petite older woman with light blond hair and purple scrubs. Her expression appeared friendly enough as she checked my vitals on the screen.

"You seem to be doing better," she continued, flashing me a smile. She fiddled with something, my IV, before pulling back. "I'm sure you have some questions."

"Only a few," I said with heavy sarcasm. She smiled again, undeterred by my bitterness. Maybe she was just one of those people that always smiled, even when the world turned to shit around them.

"The doctor should arrive soon. Fortunately, we were able to operate in time to save that leg of yours." She nodded towards said leg, propped up by strings hanging from the ceiling. "We were able to stop the infection, and your wounds are healing quite nicely."

"What happened? What's going on?" I pressed my palm against my forehead, as if I would somehow be able to conjure memories back into my brain.

"The police should also be here shortly to talk to you," the nurse said, ignoring my questions.

Where are the guys? Did they make it out okay?

I didn't dare voice these questions aloud. I feared what the answer would be.

"Where are my parents?" I asked instead. Her expression darkened, eyes glimmering with sympathy.

"Unfortunately, they weren't able to stay. You've been unconscious for a while."

I hesitated, biting my bottom lip, before I blurted out what I really wanted to know. "Is there anyone waiting for me?"

Like six handsome young men?

Again, the nurse flashed me a kind smile.

"I'm sorry, hon, but with everything that has been happening..."

"It's okay," I said quickly, ignoring the bitter taste in my mouth. "I understand."

What I understood was that I was alone, again. What had I expected? For the boys to continue talking with me after they left the resort? I was a freak, a murderer, and it was no wonder they wanted nothing to do with me. Despite knowing the reasons, my stomach clenched with the loneliness that threatened to bury me alive.

I, once again, had nobody.

But hey, on the bright side, that was my longest friendship since Ducky. A solid three days, give or take.

The doctor came in right after the nurse left and reiterated what the nurse had already told me.

Lucky blah blah blah leg blah blah blah infection.

I barely paid him any mind.

After he left, I fiddled with the remote connected to the bed by a wire.

I flipped through channels absently, though most of the stations featured the same story: mysterious virus and unpredictable weather.

I focused on a news story about this.

Virus continued to baffle scientists.

No cure found.

Tsunami hits the east coast, killing hundreds.

Death count in Kansas City reaches 1,000.

Paris reporting erratic behavior by citizens.

My mind swirled with the onslaught of information. Unable to handle it all, I switched the TV off and dropped the remote.

This couldn't be happening. This type of thing just didn't happen in real life. In books, maybe. In movies, sure.

But here?

Now?

I squeezed my eyelids shut in an attempt to rid myself of the images from both the resort and television. I felt nauseous. The amount of death and violence...

I wanted the ground to swallow me whole. Anything to escape the horrors of this world. It was hell. This world was hell.

Had my past sins somehow causing this? Was that why this was happening?

That hardly seemed fair. The world shouldn't suffer because of my past transgressions.

I wished that I was smarter, better able to fully comprehend what was happening and why. Taxes and business law classes were so helpful at this moment (said no one ever). Why hadn't I been able to study the environment or pathogens?

Sighing, I turned towards the sliver of sunlight that illuminated the room through the cracked blinds. The day looked beautiful, not at all like a tornado had struck. The sun rose high in the sky, making the morning dew on the grass shine. There were a few people in the hospital courtyard that I could see, but nobody I recognized.

I tried not to be hurt by that. I really, really tried.

I SPENT three days in the hospital. Three days of monotonous procedures consisting of needles jabbing into my skin and my body being checked over thoroughly. I probably stunk something awful by the time they released me, for the damn nurse didn't allow me to shower. No, she insisted on something called a "sponge bath" - as if I was really going to let a complete stranger wipe me down.

The doctor gave me a wheelchair that my insurance paid for. I was supposed to remain in it for two weeks before I would be able to move to crutches. I hated the wheelchair with a passion. It made me feel weak, like an invalid. I understood the need, of course, what with the stitches on my arm and back prohibiting me from using crutches, but I still complained as I was wheeled outside.

My parents hadn't even bothered to pick me up. No sir, they sent the limo driver to do that. The damn limo driver. It wasn't as if I necessarily wanted to see my parents, but anything would've been better than the impassive man whose name was never given to me. Couldn't I, at least for a moment, have people that loved me? Was that too much to ask for? I supposed the bitterness stemmed from the lack of love distributed to me by my parents. There was only so much a girl could deal with before she exploded. Or imploded, whichever one you prefer.

"Where are we going?" I asked the driver after I managed to maneuver myself into the leather seat.

"A hotel," he answered stiffly. I waited for him to offer up more information, but he remained mute. He worked for my parents, so I wasn't even surprised. The employees seemed to have a clause in their contracts that demanded them to be a bitch to me, no matter the situation.

Apparently, nearly dying didn't change that mentality.

With nothing left to do, I fiddled with the lock on the door. Push in. Push out. Push in. Push out.

I pretended that I was heading home to a large, Victorian manor with sweeping pillars and a throng of trees surrounding it. I pretended that my family would be greeting me at the door, arms outstretched as they welcomed me. It was stupid, wistful thinking, but I couldn't help the daydream that I was going somewhere where I was wanted and not just tolerated.

Through the tinted windows, I watched the scenery change from roiling landscapes to toppled buildings and crushed houses. Debris coated the road, wind carrying it from its initial resting place. It appeared to be such a desolate place. I could barely connect it to the town I once knew and hated. The further away we drove from the hospital, the more I noticed trees littering the ground and one grand buildings reverted to loose wood and plaster.

Horror filled me at the destruction.

We drove for what felt like hours before the car pulled into a modest, three-story hotel with manicured grass and freshly washed windows. This hotel must've missed the majority of the destruction wrought by the tornado.

"Thank you," I said to the driver, opening the door. He, of course, ignored me.

It was difficult to seat myself back in the wheelchair. Mr. Driver Asshole refused to help me, so I settled for awkwardly jamming my elbow into the doorframe and then accidentally rolling the chair down a hill.

Fun times.

By the time I finally made it inside, a suitcase of my belongings planted firmly on my lap, I had managed to run into three walls and two doors. How the latter had happened, when I only needed to enter one door, was a true testament of my skills.

In my defense, I hadn't known that the door wouldn't open automatically. Seriously. What was the point of the blue handicap button if it didn't work?

The manager of this hotel, employed under my father, handed me a room key. I didn't bother asking where I would be staying; I just didn't care anymore.

I didn't care about anything.

Wheeling myself into the elevator, I ignored the angry looks I received from the guests as the chair took up their precious space in the small box. Those lazy fuckers could've walked up the staircase. They weren't in a wheelchair.

The elevator pinged at the second floor, and I successfully maneuvered myself into the hallway. I heard one of my fellow elevator riders mutter something under his breath that sounded like "finally", and I flipped him off.

The sparsely lit hallway had horrible, flowered wallpaper and burgundy carpeting. Just looking at it made me want to vomit.

My room, of course, was the furthest one down the hall. I struggled to wheel myself around the corner, and then struggled yet again to actual fit through the doorway. Were doors always this small?

By the time I made it inside the room, I was utterly exhausted. On the bright side, I didn't need to work out ever again. Nope, this girl could eat all the chocolate she wanted to compensate for such a rigorous workout.

Yay me. Small victories.

I surveyed the small room, noting with glee the single bed on the plush carpeting. I wasn't ready to face my parents yet. I didn't think I would ever be ready. The room was simple: a desk, leather chair, mini-fridge, microwave, and a bathroom. The plainness of the room did not deter me as it would've my parents. I much preferred this lightly furnished room than the elaborate designs back at the resort.

This hotel, I knew, was part of a chain owned by my dear parents. I hadn't been to this specific one, but I had been to one similar.

Daddy called this his "dump". The employees were his "dumpers", and the guests were the "garbage". My dad was a very eloquent man, mind you.

Throwing myself onto the quilted bed, I allowed my mind to think over everything that had happened. Those thoughts only brought tiny pinpricks of terror, all surrounding six certain men. What happened to them? I had jumped to the conclusion that they wanted nothing to do with me, but what if I was wrong? What if they had been hurt? Or died?

What if they were still trapped beneath the resort?

If that was the case, then that would make me a shitty friend. Friends don't let friends get trapped beneath resorts. Wasn't that common sense?

Groaning, I pulled at my greasy hair in anger and frustration.

I didn't want to think about the guys. Either option was not pleasant. I would much prefer the guys to have decided that they hated me than for them to still be trapped. I would have even preferred for them to decide that Elena would be better suited as their sister that wasn't a sister instead of me.

Anything was better than the alternative.

Muffling my scream with a pillow, I emptied my mind. It was easier that way.

I didn't want to feel the pain.

I did, however, want to feel the water from a shower. How to get there...?

~

"Fucking shit. Damn dick sucking bitch. Fuck."

Trying to move in a wheelchair is difficult to say the least. Trying to move in a wheelchair in the middle of the night is damn near impossible.

After many new bruises and curse words - and one near death experience involving a pool - I made my way to the back of the hotel.

I hadn't had a direction in mind when I began my aimless wander. I just wanted to get out. Out of the room, out of my head, out of my life. Somehow, my feet (wheels) found themselves at the back lot of the hotel, next to an abandoned basketball court and a play-set.

It was creepy back here so late. The crescent moon provided very little light. But the air was refreshing, and the pungent smell of lilacs made me sigh in relief. Anything, and I meant anything, was better than staying in the stuffy confines of that room.

That was, of course, until a twig snapped in the distance.

I froze, hands clenched over top of my wheels. I may have been a speed demon, but damn it, there were too many walls for me not to hit at least one of them if I had to escape.

Now, you might think that it was completely idiotic to go outside when there was a mysterious virus or drug or whatever. In my defense, I hadn't expected anything to be inside the gates of the hotel.

And, to be completely honest, I never really planned through my decisions until after I was dealing with the consequences. It's only then that I would look back and realize that I had messed the fuck up.

Healthy, I know.

Slowly, as to not to alert whoever was here with me that I was retreating, I wheeled myself backwards. Of course, an ear-splitting squeak erupted from the chair.

Of course.

Because things couldn't just go smoothly for once, could it? Get it? Smoothly? Because of the chair...oh, never mind.

Maybe whoever was here, whoever was lurking in the shadows of the swing-set, wouldn't see me. Maybe I could escape back through the door unnoticed.

Just as I thought this, a small figure hurled at me, hissing.

I squeaked, a decidedly pathetic attempt at a scream if I wanted someone to hear me, and used my arms as a protective shield for my face.

The fur ball jumped onto my lap and-

Fur?

I slowly lowered my hands and stared at the offending creature. The cat's fur was matted to its head, dark rivulets of blood cascading down its nose. One look, and I determined that the cat was a boy.

Pushing away my unease, I used my finger to scratch behind its ear. The cat purred.

"What are you doing out here? Where's your owner?" I cooed in a high-pitched voice that made me wince. Apparently, I turned into an Elena when it came to animals.

I felt along the cat's neck.

"You have no collar boy. Where did you come from?"

I waited, actually waited, as if the cat was going to answer me. Sometimes I really did question my sanity.

"You are filthy, do you know that?"

Suddenly, the cat lurched to its feet on my lap and turned towards the playset. The hairs on his back stood on end, and he began hissing yet again.

"What's the matter, boy?" I asked softly, petting beneath his chin. Unlike before, the cat did not calm with my touch. He continued to stare at the thicket of trees surrounding the playground. It was almost as if...as if...

As if there was someone there.

Like cold water had been poured down my shirt, I tucked the cat closer against my chest with one hand. With my other hand, I began to roll back towards the door.

I didn't dare look behind me, look towards where the cat was still hissing. I didn't want to see what was out there. I didn't even want to know.

Using my key card, I quickly scrambled back inside, the wheel from my chair nearly getting stuck on the rug.

The cat, now that we were inside, seemed to calm considerably. He kneaded my lap with his tiny feet before curling up into a ball.

I petted his back absently, but my eyes couldn't help but wander towards the window next to the door.

At first, I didn't see anything. I had thought maybe I had imagined the whole thing. Just as I was about to turn away, something stepped into the thin shaft of moonlight.

Taking in its torn ear and the wagging tail, I realized it was a dog. A freaking dog. Suddenly, the cat's behavior made sense, and it made me feel like an idiot. I almost laughed at myself and my paranoia. I watched the dog take a few steps closer, now standing underneath the hotel's outdoor lights. The laughter died in my throat.

On closer inspection, I saw the dog's eyes were a bright, vivid red. Blood red. Something white was foaming at its mouth.

Well shit.

CHAPTER 17

I named the cat My Only Friend, or Mof for short. I was pleased to find, after an intense scrub down, that Mof had fur as black as night, like molten obsidian stones. I know some people believe that black cats were a sign of bad luck, but come on. Have you ever seen one before?

They're freaking adorable.

Shaking out his wet fur, Mof made himself comfortable on the edge of my bed. I never had a pet before, and I didn't know the first thing to do with him. Should I search for his owner? Buy him a collar?

Feed him?

Yes, I should definitely feed him.

Reaching into my duffle bag, I grabbed my phone and charger. I hadn't looked at the damn thing in days, not since I received the text message from Dad instructing me to go to the lobby. I really sucked at owning a phone.

"Don't worry, handsome man," I said to Mof, scratching behind his ears. "I'm going to look up what I can and can't feed you until I'm able to get to the store and buy you kitty food. Does that sound good?"

Yes, I was talking to the cat. Yes, I knew it was pathetic. And yes, I most definitely did not care. As the name implied, Mof was my only friend.

I awkwardly leaned over the bed, as I didn't want to grab my wheelchair, to plug in my phone. I was pretty proud of myself when I didn't face-plant onto the ground.

"I think that we're going to be good friends," I told the cat seriously. "I don't really have a lot of them. I thought I had some, but it seems I was mistaken. But you and me? We're going to be inseparable. You heard me right. Just you and me..."

I trailed off as Mof hopped off the bed and ran into the bathroom. Apparently even the cat got tired of me.

Dejection settled over me like a heavy cloak.

Why did I have to feel this way? Where was the light at the end of the tunnel?

The ping of my phone interrupted my admittedly depressing thoughts.

I frowned at the intrusion. Who would be calling me?

That sound was immediately followed up by dozens upon dozens of more beeps. Text messages, apparently, and a lot of them at that.

My frown deepened as I listened to my phone go off. I knew for a fact that it wasn't my parents; they gave less shits about me than I did. Nobody else even had my number that I was aware of, except for maybe their head of security. But why would the dick call or message me?

Nearly tumbling off the bed yet again, I picked up my phone from where it lay charging on the ground. The phone cord did not quite reach my bed, so I was forced to lean over the edge, balancing precariously on my side.

Unknown: Addie, please respond.

I didn't recognize the number, but there were at least fifty from it. Mixed in were several other numbers, though I didn't recognize any of those either. Frowning, I scrolled through the onslaught of text messages.

Unknown 1: Calax gave me your number. Please text back.

Unknown 2: this is rider. R u okay?

Unknown 3: Princess, please message back. We're losing our shit over here.

The messages went on and on, each one more desperate than the last. I scrolled to the end of the chain, to the most recent messages and felt tears threaten to break free. The time stamp on the first I opened said it had been sent only five minutes ago.

Unknown 1: I don't know if you're getting these. I don't think so. I'm so sorry. Calax lost his damn mind, and Declan's turned into a scary mofo. I don't know if you're getting these and not able to respond, or if something else happened. I refuse to believe that something worse happened, so please respond. Please.

And the last text, dated only two minutes earlier.

Unknown: I love you, baby. I'm sorry.

A sob escaped me, and then I was crying, nearly hysterical. I'm ashamed to admit that I wailed like a toddler as I read through the texts. Again. And again.

They cared. They honestly cared. And Calax - I knew it was Calax without a shred of doubt - loved me. My emotions were everywhere. I had always wanted somebody to love me, to care for me.

And now I had Calax.

Tears burning my eyes, I scrolled up until I found the number that I identified as Tam's. He seemed to be the sanest, at least in the consecutive texts sent in the last few days. Even Asher's messages sounded frenzied the more time went on without a response from me.

Wiping the fallen tears from my eyes, I held the phone to my ear as the line rang.

It only took one ring for the phone to pick up, voice breathless over the line.

"Addie? Kitten?" The voice wasn't Tam's, but I recognized the raspy tone immediately.

"Hi, Ryder."

A strangled sound escaped him.

"Shit, Addie...we thought...we thought you were dead." His voice turned harsher, angrier, as if he was overwhelmed with emotion and couldn't decide which one to settle on. "Why didn't you fucking call? You can't just do shit like this and not call. We thought you were fucking dead! Do you know what that did to us? To Calax and Declan? For the love of...fuck! Kitten, you should've called!" There was what sounded like a scuffle on the other end of the line before a gruff voice spoke.

"Adelaide?"

I didn't recognize this new voice. I was positive that I had never heard him before. He was not one of my new friends.

"Yes?" I began hesitantly. My lip gnawed on my fingernail. It was a very nasty habit that I have been determined to break.

"Give us your location. We'll be there soon."

There was a pause. Slightly muffled, as if his hand was over the receiver, the man said, "Calm the fuck down, Ryder. You'll see her soon. Go grab the others and try to find Calax."

Deciding quickly, I rattled off the hotel's address. I didn't give him my room number, in case he was a psycho murderer.

Or - wait for it - a cat burglar.

I looked down at Mof smugly as I thought of that pun.

"I'm not a murderer or a cat burglar," he said in exasperation. I didn't even know him, yet I knew his eyes were rolling.

Squeaking, I quickly mumbled a "bye" before hanging up. I threw the phone against the wall as if it was the phone's fault I was a fuck up.

Yup. Totally blaming the phone.

I let out a very girly giggle.

They cared about me. They actually cared. And Calax...

I thought about his text message. I didn't know how I felt about his impromptu confession. Doubt nagged me. Did he mean it, or were those words said in a panic? I didn't know which one I wanted to be true.

Did I love Calax? Maybe. After Ducky, I wasn't sure I was even capable of love. Calax was a grouchy bastard on the best of days, but he had always been there for me. Since the first day we'd met, he had never given up on me, despite the awful things I said to him.

I hated him. I told myself that I hated him, yet my heart said something else entirely. I didn't understand what it meant, but I knew that I would be forever changed with this realization.

And that was why I didn't do feelings. They sucked.

After a few unsuccessful tries, I was finally able to scoop up Mof and wheel myself to the elevator. I decided to wait in the lobby for the boys.

It was nearly empty when I arrived, minus the front desk clerk I had met earlier. He eyed me with obvious distaste when I entered but seemed to realize I didn't intend to intrude on his phone time and lost his scowl. He didn't even reprimand me for having Mof, despite the hotel's no pets allowed policy.

Placing myself in front of the fireplace, I allowed the dancing flames to warm my frigid hands. It wasn't cold in the hotel by any means, but I felt as if my body had been plunged into the Arctic Ocean in the middle of winter. Chilled. I felt chilled, if not slightly numb.

At the swish of the door opening, my head snapped up, eager to lay eyes on the guys. I was momentarily disappointed when only a single, unfamiliar male stepped into the lobby. That disappointment morphed into curiosity when his gaze landed on me, and he walked swiftly in my direction.

He was tall, almost as tall as Calax, with clearly defined muscles displayed in a fitted black t-shirt and black sweats. His shoulder-length, brown hair was pulled back into a ponytail, and he had the prettiest brown eyes I had ever seen. Normally, I wouldn't think brown eyes were pretty. The color reminded me too much of mud. But his eyes were different, almost as if they were infused with gold. They stood out against his tanned skin.

He was ridiculously attractive, and he was staring at me.

I stupidly looked over my shoulder to see if there was someone behind me before focusing again on the tall man before me.

"Adelaide?" he asked, voice clipped. I, once again, looked around. Nope, no other Adelaide's were offering themselves up.

"Yes, and you are?"

He didn't offer me a hand, and I didn't offer him mine. We continued our stare-off, the air around us practically crackling with electricity. I refused to look away first.

"Fallon," he answered. Again, briskly.

I raised an eyebrow.

"And that name is supposed to mean something to me because...?"

Before "Fallon" could speak, a figure ran through the doorway and threw himself at my feet. Mof hissed, but settled down when the newcomer didn't come near his resting place on my lap.

"Don't you dare do something like that again!" Ryder began, a flurry of emotions distorting his features before he finally settled on relieved. "You scared the shit out of me, Kitten. Why didn't you call and tell us you were fine? Were you trying to give us a damn heart attack? Shit, you can't do stuff like that-"

"Calm down, Ryder," Fallon said gruffly. Ryder glared at the other guy.

"Fuck off, Sarge."

Sarge. So this was the mysterious Sarge. The group leader. The guy capable of rescuing his team after a tornado trapped them underground.

What made him so impressive?

His cold eyes narrowed on me.

Oops. Must've spoken aloud.

Ryder let out a sound that was a cross between a chuckle and a sob. He looked as if he wanted to hug me but wasn't sure where he could touch me with all the bandages. I probably resembled a mummy.

"Did you get ahold of the others?" Fallon asked, turning away from me to level his glare on Ryder. Unlike me, Ryder seemed unperturbed. Perhaps he was just used to it.

"I found Tam. He's tracking down the others right now. I haven't been able to talk to Calax yet."

"Calax?" His name caused my heart to beat unevenly. "Why wouldn't you be able to get ahold of him? Where is he?"

I wanted to talk to Calax more than I ever wanted to talk to anyone in my life. I didn't understand these emotions, but I didn't shy away from them. I wouldn't - couldn't - after everything that had happened. Death, and the consequential loneliness, changed my perspective on a lot of things.

"We'll explain everything," Ryder said. His hand reached forward as if he wanted to touch me, before he quickly dropped it back onto his lap. I hated seeing Ryder so tentative, so unsure. I grabbed his wrist and brought his hand to my face.

I didn't understand his need to touch me, only that he did. A slight tremor went through his body, and his eyes shut. His thumb stroked my cheekbone.

"Come on. We need to get back," said Fallon, eyes fixed on Ryder's hand. An almost contemplative expression crossed his handsome features before it hardened yet again.

"Will you come back with us?" Ryder asked me. His eyes remained closed, but a tranquil smile made him look years younger. I liked this Ryder more than the other one, the cocky, flirty one. There was something real and vulnerable about him that had been absent in our previous interactions.

I hesitated as I considered Ryder's request.

"Please." His eyes snapped open. "Calax needs to see you with his own eyes. And Declan...please?"

It was the final please that did me in. I was a sucker for puppy dog eyes.

"Fine, but only if Mof can come too."

He titled his head in confusion.

"Who the fuck is Mof...and when the fuck did you get a cat?"

CHAPTER 18

*S*arge was not a talkative person.

I realized that as we piled into a black sedan. Despite the available front seat, Ryder insisted that he had to sit beside me. He kept touching my hand and shoulder, as if he was reassuring himself that I was there and alive.

At first, the constant contact made me almost uncomfortable. Maybe uncomfortable was too strong of a word, but it wasn't something I was used to. I'd only ever had bad experiences with physical contact, making it difficult for me not to shy away.

After the fifth touch, I realized that I enjoyed his hand in mine. It brought me comfort, something that I had been severely lacking for years now.

"What happened?" I asked as Sarge - Fallon - pulled out of the parking lot. "How did we get out?"

How did I survive? I thought but didn't say.

Ryder idly played with my fingers as he spoke, his voice steadily becoming more excited as the story continued. He reminded me of an energetic little boy bouncing around (though I would never dare call him a little boy to his face).

"Well, Sarge here realized that we were still in the resort when it collapsed. He hoped that we would be smart enough to make it to a lower level. They found the majority of people on the level just above ours. But Sarge didn't give up. No, he got an entire crew to help dig us out. They came in guns blazing."

Ryder paused, a forlorn expression marring his handsome face. Fallon merely grunted. I figured that the man, the Sargent, had talked himself out with our earlier conversation. All he managed now were noncommittal murmurs and growls. A man of few words, I guess.

"How many casualties were there?" I asked softly, though I dreaded the answer. Ryder squeezed my hand.

"Thirty-seven."

I told myself that the number wasn't that bad. That it could've been higher. It felt wrong to think like that, but I knew I would fall apart at the seams if I allowed myself to think of the people that had died. Right now, I could compartmentalize the losses. They were nameless characters with no stories. I didn't want to know any details about them; I couldn't bear the truth.

"What about the people with us? Elena? And..."

I couldn't say his name, but my mind conjured up an image of a cold man with cropped hair and a heated glare.

Brad was a monster straight from my nightmares. Ironically, I couldn't help the thought that the only beings that had ever hurt me were humans.

Monsters did exist, and they too often took the forms of the ones we thought we could trust the most.

"Brad didn't make it," Ryder said, eyes dark. Both relief and dread filled me at that proclamation. On one hand, I was grateful I would never see his murderous face again. On the other, he was still a person with a story and a life, possibly a family. He might've had a wife and children. He for sure was the son of someone, perhaps even a brother.

And now he was gone. Another person in this fucked-up world that ceased to exist.

"How did he die?" The words came out before I could censor them.

Ryder answered simply, "Shannon."

I didn't ask what happened to the blond waitress. I had a feeling I already knew the answer if the tightening of Ryder's jaw was any indication.

We rode for a while in silence. Ryder would occasionally glance over at me, as if he was assessing how I was holding up.

"Have you eaten anything today?" Ryder whispered after a moment. "Besides hospital food?"

I considered lying to him, but there didn't seem to be any point.

"No," I admitted back, just as quietly.

Before I could add that I wasn't hungry, which would've been a lie, Ryder leaned over the center console.

"Can we stop and get some fast-food? Kitten here is hungry."

My cheeks blushed at the nickname, especially when Fallon's inquisitive eyes met mine in the rearview mirror. I had the distinct feeling that this man missed nothing.

He did what I had come to expect from him: grunted an affirmative.

Taking a road that curved steeply up ahead, Fallon pulled the car in front of a familiar restaurant. The Golden Arches were easily recognizable.

Despite only being nine o'clock, not a single light was on. The parking lot was empty of any car besides ours.

"That's odd," Ryder said, echoing my thoughts. Without a word, Fallon pulled back onto the road.

Since we were now off the highway, I was finally able to see the town that we were in. It was odd, but it appeared to be almost abandoned. No restaurant or store was open, and the houses, nestled between businesses at intermittent intervals, had the blinds drawn closed and lights off

It suddenly occurred to me how few cars were on the road. Even at this late hour, there should've been more than the handful I had spotted.

An uneasy feeling made the hairs on the back of my neck stand on end. My hand tightened in Mof's fur. The kitten continued to snuggle in my lap, completely oblivious. What I wouldn't give to be a cat right about now.

"I'm not that hungry," I hurried to say. I felt unreasonably frightened, though by what, I couldn't discern.

Fallon made a noise, but he maneuvered the car back onto the highway. I counted, in the time it took us to get to wherever we were going, five cars in total. Five cars on the highway.

The uneasy feeling transformed into full-on terror.

Something wasn't right.

"Where are we going?" I asked, relieved when my voice didn't tremble over those few words.

"Since the resort's out of commission, we've been staying at Sarge's," Ryder supplied, offering me a sympathetic smile at the first part of his statement. I realized then that I should've been mourning not only the loss of life, but the loss of my home.

I found that I couldn't even summon a single tear for the damn place. The bad memories far outweighed the good ones.

"You have a bunch of teenage boys staying with you?" I asked Fallon, focusing on the last part of Ryder's statement. "No wonder you don't talk much. I would be a brooding asshole too if I had to deal with these idiots 24/7."

"Hey!" Ryder said in mock-offense, but I thought I saw a hint of a smile cross Fallon's impassive face.

It was small, but it was there. I would call that a win, especially since Fallon didn't strike me as a smiling type of person. More like a murder-you-in-your-sleep type person.

He was a scary motherfucker, that was for sure.

I don't know what I expected his house to be like, but a modest, two-story home with a white-picket fence wasn't it. It was the type of house you would expect a suburban family to live in.

Unless...

"Holy shit! Do you have kids?" I asked Fallon in disbelief. He didn't look that much older than me, mid-twenties at most, but who was I to judge the accuracy of the sex organ? He might've hit bullseyes every time for all I knew.

"You did not just say the accuracy of the sex organ," Ryder groaned. I shrugged in response. He didn't have to listen to my inner mumblings.

Another one of those diminutive smiles graced Fallon's features.

"No kids," he answered.

I eyed him quizzically.

"Girlfriend? Wife? Boyfriend? Husband? Come on man, this is such a soccer mom home."

Ryder broke into laughter at my description, and Fallon looked towards the heavens. He wouldn't find the patience to deal with me up there. I was more associated with the other place.

"I think she's calling you a granny," Ryder said to Fallon between fits of laughter. To me, he said, "I've been trying to tell this bastard that his house is not a suitable bachelor pad, but he doesn't ever fucking listen to me."

Ignoring him, Fallon walked to the trunk and grabbed my wheelchair. Unlike the asshole limo driver, Fallon and Ryder both helped me settle into the chair before pushing me up the gravel driveway. Fallon grabbed Mof for me, and the cat snuggled into his arms. I smiled at the sight of a muscular, scary-ass man cooing at a kitten.

My smile grew when I spotted rows of perfectly planted perennials along the edge of the house.

Yup. Totally a granny house. All it would need next was some cherub statues to complete the old person feel.

Ryder sent me an amused glance at my ramblings while Fallon glared.

I noted, with some satisfaction, that the glare didn't hold near as much contempt as it previously had. Instead of full-on hating me, he appeared to rather full-on tolerate me. Trust me. There was a big difference.

Ryder and Fallon were forced to carry me and my chair up the front steps. He really should invest in a ramp. Hell, the entire world needed more ramps. We should just have ramps everywhere. And-

Getting off track again, Addie.

"Yup," Fallon muttered.

Fuck off.

The interior of the house was in sharp contrast to the exterior. Here, the resemblance to a granny-pad ended. Leather couches made up the living room, complete with a large flat screen and a few gaming devices. The kitchen, to the right, was surprisingly clean save a few pizza boxes discarded on the counter.

All in all, it wasn't what I expected a bachelor pad to look like, especially sharing it with six other guys.

"Addie!" a jubilant voice cried. "Princess!"

Ronan appeared from the top of the staircase, a towel around his shoulders. He was wearing low-slung shorts that showed the irresistible Adonis belt I found so attractive on guys. Like the first time I saw him, his unicorn tattoo was on display, large and proud. I had to wonder about the meaning of that tattoo.

"Hi, Lucky Charms," I greeted him as he jumped down the remaining steps. His arms immediately engulfed me, and I resisted the urge to wince.

Fallon, however, must've noticed my discomfort, for he grabbed Ronan by the arm and jerked him away from me.

"Careful of her injuries," he barked. He reminded me so much of Calax in that moment that I couldn't help my smile. That smile instantly faded when my heart began pounding. I felt...anxious to see him again. Anxious and something else, something new.

Shaking my head to clear my muddled thoughts, I smiled up at Ronan to show that he hadn't hurt me, and I wasn't mad. "Where are the others?"

"We're here."

The voice belonged to Asher, the first, excluding Calax and Ducky, of the boys that I had met. The sweet, shy boy that had seemed so flirtatious that night at the restaurant. Now, he just stared down at me with wide, glossy eyes.

"I'm glad you're okay, Sweetheart," he said softly. Tam, behind him, took a step towards me and squeezed my hand. He didn't make eye-contact with me, and he didn't speak any words, but that was okay. I understood all that he tried to convey in that single gesture. I had been worried about him too.

"Where's Ducky and Calax?"

"Declan's in the dining room, and we don't know where Calax is," Ronan said.

"How do you not know where he is?" I asked in horror. A thousand scenarios ran through my head, each one worse than the next.

Asher rubbed my shoulder reassuringly. "Don't worry. We'll find him." He paused, considering his words carefully.

"But you should talk to Declan. He...well....you should just go talk to him."

With that, Asher gave my shoulder another squeeze and nudged my chair in the direction of the dining room. When none of the guys moved to follow me or push my chair, I realized this was something I had to do alone.

What would I even say to him? Ducky had been my best friend, but Declan was a virtual stranger. How much of the long-haired, shy boy still lingered in the bitter man?

Shoving away my doubts, I tentatively rolled through the archway and into the dining room.

Declan sat at the table, profile to me. His eyes remained fixated on a single spot on the faded wallpaper.

For a moment, I sat and inspected the boy before he could see me.

The expression on his face, that distraught, horrified expression, was all Ducky's. I would remember that face anywhere; it was the same one he gave me the night of my thirteenth birthday. The night everything changed for both of us.

I honestly couldn't tell you how I felt about the realization that Declan was Ducky. I was surprised, sure, but I was also wary. A lot had changed in those few years. I had changed, and I knew Declan had as well. Would we still be compatible as friends? After everything I did, would he even want to be mine?

That last thought haunted me. If I were to admit it to myself, that was a driving factor in my hesitance to pursue a friendship with Declan. A part of me felt I didn't deserve his friendship, despite his reassurances that I did. Guilt was a funny thing.

I also didn't know if I was supposed to be mad at him or not. He left me believing he was dead, but, in his defense, he thought I hadn't cared. I believed that fact hurt me most of all. How could he not know how much I loved him?

Moving slowly, so to not startle him, I rested my hand on his bicep. Declan jerked under my touch, eyes coming up to glare...

Only for a mask to fall over his face, becoming completely unreadable.

For a moment, he simply stared at me. His eyes traced each of my features as if he wanted to commit them to memory.

And then he began to sob. Mr. Glarey, the boy I once believed to be nothing but an asshole, began to cry in earnest. His hands fumbled, reaching for my own, and I grabbed onto both of his in both of mine. I don't know how long we sat there holding one another, but it didn't feel like long enough.

We had years to catch up on, and I was determined not to lose any more time with him than I already had.

CHAPTER 19

When nightfall came, and Calax still had not arrived, I felt myself panicking. Where could he be?

I could tell by the tense faces of the other guys that they, too, were worried.

Okay, let's think this through, Addie. What do you know about Calax? He likes control, that much is obvious. And what else? He likes you. Correction, he loves you. Think, Addie. Think.

"Don't knock yourself out," Ronan said from where he was sprawled out on the couch. I leveled at him my best glare. Sadly, my glare resembled Mof's glare more than anything scary.

"He thought you were dead, Sweetie," Tam said gently, and I blinked at the term of endearment. He hurried on, "Do you know where he would go to feel close to you?"

I thought that through. If what he said was true, if Calax was grieving over my supposed death, than it would stand to reason that he would want to feel connected with me somehow. Where would I go if I wanted to remember Calax?

The answer came to me easily, and I could've facepalmed myself for not realizing it sooner.

"Of course," I hissed. Ignoring the questioning looks from the other guys, I turned to Fallon. "I think I have an idea where Calax went."

"Care to share with the class, Princess?" Ronan asked.

"Where we met. His house."

DESPITE THE BOYS' protests, Fallon refused to allow any of them to accompany us. I could tell that didn't sit well with any of them, especially Declan. My old best friend glared at Fallon with an almost elemental fury. I was not wrong in my initial assessment that Declan was a scary motherfucker when he wanted to be.

Ignoring him - and Ryder who insisted that we were car buddies - Fallon wheeled me to the sedan. Unlike before, I was able to claim shotgun.

"So, Sargent," I mused. "Like the army guy?"

"That's Sergeant," Fallon said roughly. "And yes, I am that as well, but my last name is, ironically enough, Sargent. Spelled S-A-R-G-E-N-T." He glanced at me as if I was an idiot – but really, how was I supposed to know his last fucking name was spelled differently when it was pronounced the same way?

I didn't bother with small-talk after that as we curved through the winding roads of the town. I knew Sarge wouldn't be receptive to any communication outside the occasional grunt and snorts. I had to admit that it took a very special person to create his own language.

Fallon snorted beside me (case in point), and I realized I must've spoken aloud. Oh well. You win some; you lose some.

After what felt like hours, but I knew was only a few minutes, Fallon pulled the car into an apartment complex that looked as if it had seen better days. Though not completely destroyed, a tree leaned precariously against the white siding, and glass now took up residence in the once thriving garden. I would know since I was the one who had planted it.

Long story.

"He's probably not up in his room," I mused to Fallon who, of course, didn't respond.

At least I hoped Calax hadn't been stupid enough to climb up three sets of stairs to his room. That building looked as if it was going to fall apart at any moment, and I really didn't want to get trapped again.

Or sacrificed. I didn't want that either.

Fortunately, I spotted the silhouette kneeling near the pond. I wasn't surprised to find him at that particular spot.

After all, it was where we had our first, and only, kiss.

"Stay here," I instructed Fallon. He glared at him, not used to taking orders, but remained where he was after he helped me into my chair.

The headlights from the car illuminated the paved trail down to the pond. Despite this, I still managed to get my chair stuck on a rock and face-plant into the granite. Okay, so it may have been more of a pebble than a rock, but that shit hurt! Fallon, laughing like the bastard he was, got out of the car, helped me back into my chair, and then retreated to lean against the bumper.

"Go away!" Calax bellowed as I got near. "I don't want to talk to any of you!"

I had never heard his voice sound quite like that before. I had heard him growling, and I had heard him upset, but I had never heard him sound so...empty before. From the hunching of his shoulders, it almost appeared as if he had given up.

I didn't like that.

Calax was supposed to be the brave and fearless leader, for that I was what I always perceived him as. The sudden change from a prowling tiger to a shriveling boy scared me a little.

"If you wanted me to leave, you only had to ask nicely. No need to be an ass," I snarked, coming to sit beside him. His head whipped in my direction, back towards the pond, and then towards me again in a dramatic double-take. It would've been comical if there hadn't been tears in his eyes.

"Addie?" His voice was so soft I almost didn't hear it. "Baby?"

"It's me, Callie," I said.

Instead of the relief I expected, Calax began to laugh. Like full on, clutch your stomach and fall to the ground type of laughter. Way to make a girl feel wanted. He needed to up his game.

"What's so funny?" I demanded. I really didn't appreciate being the butt of the joke. I much preferred the face of it.

Focus, Addie.

"You still speak your thoughts," he said, wiping tears from his eyes. "I didn't think my imagination would be that creative."

Imagination? Oh, hell no.

"I'm not your imagination, Big Guy. I'm flesh and blood. I'm a real girl now. The girl-Pinocchio."

He chuckled again, turning his head to stare at me directly. From this position, the moonlight illuminated his features in a pale glow.

He looked like shit, and not the sexy kind either.

Not that shit could be sexy. But Calax could, and I always claimed he looked like shit, so I supposed...

Stop. Thinking.

Even in the semi-darkness, I could see the deep bags

under his eyes. His face held the evidence of a beard, dark like his hair and prickly. I wondered when he had last shaved. Or showered. Or did anything, really, besides mope around and hallucinate me.

I wondered if he jacked off to my image. I wondered if he-

I really needed to just get a new brain. That would be much easier.

"Did I die?" Calax asked. "Is this Heaven?"

I couldn't help but smile. I was flattered that he thought of being with me as the equivalent to Heaven. Flattered...and a little scared. Not of Calax, but of the feelings he brought out in me.

"Trust me. You wouldn't make it there," I teased, swatting his shoulder. "Now what do I have to do to convince you that I am real?"

"You're dead. I saw your body as the paramedics took you away. I saw..." he broke off, dropping his face into his hands. I hated seeing him like this. He was my grouchy giant, not my depressed one. Gah. Even in my not-real-death, he still found ways to irritate me. I really wanted to decapitate Calax with a piece of paper at this moment. It would've been one hell of a papercut.

"I'm not fucking dead, you idiot! But you're going to be if you don't calm down."

He still looked doubtful, face pensive, so I did the only thing I could think to do.

I kissed him.

For a moment, he froze beneath me, and I wondered if I had read his text wrong. Maybe he meant that he loved me as a sister, and I was performing, in his mind, some serious incestual action here. Maybe the text wasn't even meant for me-

His large hand cupped the back of my neck, tangling in

my hair. He lips moved hungrily over mine as he thoroughly ravaged my mouth. Tiny licks of fire danced across my skin with each and every stroke of his hand. His tongue tentatively touched my bottom lip, demanding entrance, and I happily complied.

His arms were incredibly gentle as they rested on either side of me in the wheelchair. It reminded me of the way my parents regarded fine chinaware: something precious and extremely valuable.

His kisses turned soft, light brushes of lips to mine.

"Addie." He said my name reverently. Total ego booster.

"Callie."

"You're alive."

"No shit." I couldn't stop the dorky smile from taking over my face. "And you *love* me."

I had the pleasure of watching as pink tinted his cheeks. One of his large hand went to rub the back of his neck. "Not the most romantic way to confess your love for someone, but I suppose I'll accept it just this once," I teased.

At this, another smile graced his handsome features. "Are you planning on a lot of boys confessing their love to you?"

I shrugged. "You never know. I'm a very lovable person."

His eyes suddenly turned serious, all previous traces of teasing gone.

"Addie," he said, and I held my breath. "I love you. I've loved you for years. God, I just…I love the shit out of you, baby."

I opened my mouth to say it back, I honestly did, but the words got stuck. It wasn't because I didn't feel them, but more so because the thought of laying myself out there, making myself vulnerable like that, terrified me. Calax had the ability to completely shatter my heart, and with it, the last of my humanity. I wouldn't be able to survive another heartbreak.

"You don't have to say anything right now," Calax murmured, hand smoothing down my hair. "I don't expect you to."

"You have to understand that it's not because I don't feel the same way," I whispered, ashamed of my cowardice. "It's just..."

"Scary. I understand that."

How was it possible that someone was able to make me feel the way he did? I felt so much love towards this man before me, so much affection. Ducky may have been my first friend, but Calax had always been my sun. The darkness would've consumed me long ago if it hadn't been for him.

"Who the hell is that?" Calax said suddenly, glancing at something over my shoulder.

"Fallon probably," I responded, but Calax was already shaking his head.

"It's a group of people. I don't recognize them."

I finally looked over my shoulder at what Calax was seeing. It appeared to be a group of at least twenty people, all running in our direction. I couldn't make out any individual faces, but the man in front appeared to have dreadlocks.

"We need to go!" Fallon shouted suddenly. He materialized behind Calax, frantic eyes scanning our surroundings.

"What's going on?" Calax asked gruffly. Gone was the teary-eyed man that had kissed me with so much passion and love. This boy was much more familiar. A predator. I was grateful that my Calax was back. As much as I enjoyed the attention, I much preferred his assholeishness.

"The virus! Those things are coming!" Fallon gestured towards the mob growing nearer. Their movements were jerky, as if they weren't quite used to walking. The only word appropriate to describe it would be a lurch. They were lurching towards us, propelling themselves off the balls of their feet.

"The Ragers," I whispered, horrified.

"Ragers?" Calax questioned but seemed to decide we had more important issues than my choice of words. "Come on! Go! Go!"

We moved back up the hill at a brisk pace. After my wheelchair got stuck for the third time, Calax scooped me into his arms and began to run. The poor wheelchair was left behind.

Fallon began accelerating before the door of the sedan was even fully closed. I fell forward, wincing as my head hit the back of his seat. Calax grabbed my body and held me firmly against him.

"Faster," he growled. Fallon didn't respond, but the car jerked forward yet again as he pressed down on the gas.

The group had finally caught up with us. The car headlights, though dim, could clearly showcase each one of their disfigured faces. Red eyes. Black veins. Peeling skin.

I watched in horror as two Ragers began fighting each other. I didn't know what set them off, but I couldn't look away once they started. They clawed at each other's faces and bit any bare skin available. Even when blood dripped from open wounds, they didn't stop fighting.

The apparent leader, Dreadlocks, jumped onto the hood of the car. His feral eyes roamed over each of our faces before settling on mine. His lips pulled back to reveal blood-soaked teeth.

"Sarge," Calax warned darkly. The mob was surrounding our car now. Their grotesque faces were smushed against the window as their hands grappled desperately with the door handles. Even through the steel barrier, I could still hear their cries.

"Come out!"

"Feed us!"

"We're hungry!"

An horrified shudder shook my body, and Calax's arms tightened around me. It would've been painful if I hadn't been in desperate need of the comfort.

"Sarge!" This was said sharply.

Squeezing my eyelids closed, I heard and felt, rather than saw, the car drive over bodies.

Drove over fucking bodies.

The sickening crunch made my insides tighten.

Oh god no.

No. No. No.

The guttural screams became more and more distant the faster we drove, but it still wasn't enough. There would never be enough distance between me and them.

CHAPTER 20

RONAN

I glanced anxiously at the door for the third time in the last minute.

What the fuck was taking them so long? I hoped Cal would stop being such a brooding asshole and get the fuck back here. I was worried about Princess. It wasn't safe for her to be outside for so long.

Sarge had been able to get ahold of the base a couple of days ago. Apparently, they were just as clueless about everything that was happening as we were. That realization did not sit well with me. Hell, weren't the powers above supposed to be almighty and all-knowing? Fuck them. And fuck Calax.

I resumed my nervous pacing, bare feet wearing a hole in the carpet. I had never been one to sit still, and that was especially true whenever I experienced any strong emotion.

Damn Calax. Why did he have to go and run off? Didn't he realize how much danger he was putting her in?

I told myself that my concern for her was normal. After all, we were friends.

I had always wanted to meet the beauty that tamed the beast. Calax would not shut up about this girl who'd stolen his heart. Now that I'd met her, I understood why.

She was beautiful, sure, but Elena was beautiful. Beauty wasn't all there was to a person, despite Ryder's claims. Addie made me laugh. I couldn't remember the last time I had laughed before Addie came into my life. Believe it or not, it wasn't often. I was usually considered even grumpier than Calax.

But she...

She understood my weird sense of humor. Not even Ryder, my best friend and half-brother, fully understood my sarcasm and dry wit.

The devil himself was currently perched on the edge of the sofa, hands strumming absently on his guitar. If I paced when I was nervous, Ryder played. Music that is. Or females.

I didn't like the attention he gave Addie, and I didn't entirely understand why. I told myself it was because of Calax. He had been in love with her for years now; we would not get in the way of that.

It could've also been because I knew my brother. To him, females were nothing more than playthings to use and discard. I didn't want that for Princess. The mere thought of it pissed me off and made me sick to my stomach at the same time.

She had suffered so much in her short life. She deserved love and happiness, not the fuck over Ryder was bound to give her.

I had to make sure he understood that she was off limits. She was Calax's girl, and, in theory, that made me her...brother?

I shuddered at the word. No, most definitely not her

brother. Most brothers would go to jail for having thoughts about their sister like I often had for her.

Friends. We were just *friends*.

Friends protected other friends from dick-bag brothers.

And I also had Declan to think about. From the way he had talked about her, worshipped her, I knew that Calax was going to have some competition in the romance department. It was a shame that they had met her first.

"Sarge will fucking kill you if you break his rug," Ryder said absently. His hand plucked at a few strings. He used to write his own songs until that bitch Liz came into his life. She sure did a number on him.

"You can't break carpet," I retorted, resuming my pacing. His hands strummed yet again, the song unfamiliar. That was especially odd since I knew his entire set.

"Don't tell me what you can and can't break," he snapped back. Geez. Someone was in a shitty mood. I had to wonder if it had to do with his precious "Kitten".

The bastard probably wanted to fuck her.

"I hear a car!" Tamson yelled before I could respond to Ryder. Both of us rushed towards the door. Fucking Ryder looked like an energetic puppy waiting for his owner to arrive home. Pathetic. Granted, I probably looked the same way, but at least I had *some* class.

Declan came out of whichever room he was sulking in, for once not scowling. His face warmed with relief.

It was Ryder that opened the door, bouncing from foot to foot.

"Addie!" he said before the door was even fully opened. See? Puppy.

And then he froze. I could see the muscles in his back bunch together. His body thrummed with tension.

"What the fuck, Ry?" I questioned, pushing past him.

A group of people stood in the doorway. Most I didn't

recognize, but the two standing in front of the crowd were impossible to ignore.

Our target for the last few weeks. Our whole reason for being at the resort in the first place.

And the two people I hated more than anyone else in the world, including Liz (surprisingly).

The man took a step forward. With an arrogant set to his chin, he looked like an entitled dick. I wanted to punch the smile off his face.

How the hell did he even know where to find us?

"We're looking for our daughter," he said stoutly, indicating the woman next to him as if we had trouble understanding the "we". He continued, ignoring the scowl I aimed his way, "We're looking for Adelaide."

ACKNOWLEDGMENTS

There are so many people I would like to thank! First, thank you to my family: my mom, my dad, and my four amazing (*cough* annoying *cough*) siblings.

Thank you to my PA, Sosha. You have been a lifesaver.

I would also love to thank my author girls. Loxley, Lana, Chloe, Mercy, Kathryn, Jarica, Brandy, Katie, and so many more. Thank you for being rockstars guys.

And thank you Meg for editing this book! You are a superstar, and I appreciate you so much.

Finally, I would love to thank my Betas and Alphas. You ladies are amazing and have made this book what it is.

ALSO BY KATIE MAY

Together We Fall Series

1. Darkness We Crave

2. Light We Seek

3. The Storm We Face

4. The Monsters We Fight (Coming Soon)

Beyond the Shadows Series

1. Gangs and Ghosts

2. Guns and Graveyards (Coming April)

The Damning Series

1. Greed

2. Envy (Coming this Summer)

Made in the USA
Middletown, DE
04 May 2019